WHISPERS IN THE SHADOWS

PARANORMAL ENCOUNTERS OF A POLICEMAN

M.A. GANAPATHY

Srishti
PUBLISHERS & DISTRIBUTORS

Srishti Publishers & Distributors
A unit of AJR Publishing LLP
212A, Peacock Lane
Shahpur Jat, New Delhi – 110 049

editorial@srishtipublishers.com

First published by
Srishti Publishers & Distributors in 2024

10 9 8 7 6 5 4 3 2

This is a work of fiction. The characters, places, organisations and events described in this book are either a work of the author's imagination or have been used fictitiously. Any resemblance to people, living or dead, places, events, communities or organisations is purely coincidental.

Printed and bound in India.

To all the
honest Policemen...

Contents

A Note from the Author

When I was young, I was deeply fascinated by the paranormal phenomenon. My interest in the paranormal was fuelled in no small measure by the stories of certain odd events narrated by my grandfather, a retired forester, who had served in remote corners of South India. Ruskin Bond's stories in this genre became my staple at one point, which I read several times over. Kenneth Anderson, the teller of thrilling shikar tales, was another favourite of mine. I liked how he cleverly wove in shikar yarn with episodes of the occult and the supernatural. As I grew older, I ardently wished that paranormal phenomena existed, to give life on the planet one more dimension beyond the normal.

Then Covid struck the world. So many people died. Like millions, my family and I also went through the ordeal. That was when the harsh reality of human mortality and the seeming insignificance of one's own existence stared hard at my face. I thought, if I were to perish tomorrow, at least a few strangers should know that I existed on this earth. Maybe this thought was driven by pure vanity, but I wished to leave something behind in the written form with my name on it for posterity. That is because I have loved reading books all my life; they were my escape to wonderlands beyond the mundane! So, the stories in this collection were mostly visualized during the Covid times and written subsequently.

In the process, I have borrowed from Kenneth Anderson's idea mentioned earlier; but having been a policeman most of my life, I have mixed the police yarns (in most of the stories) with the paranormal. For the discerning reader, hopefully, there are underlying messages in these stories. But broadly, these stories are intended to convey some kind of wonderment and escape to the reader from the vicissitudes of a humdrum existence, while hinting towards the real possibility that there may be life beyond life as we know it! The novelty of these stories also lies in the unusual as well as diverse locations they are set in.

Having written a dozen stories and compiled them into a collection, it is my fervent hope that at least a few complete strangers will read them, and maybe, enjoy the stories, too!

I welcome you to the extraordinary encounters of Avinash, the little-known cop, whom I knew rather well!

Avinash, the little-known Policeman

Towards the end of his policing career, Avinash had become acutely aware of the fact that life's harsh realities never matched up to one's own exaggerated expectations. He was also conscious of the fact that in the nearly hundred thousand years of human existence, the overwhelming majority of people had simply disappeared into cosmic insignificance. But at the same time, he believed that while the sum total of his life's achievements seemed inconsequential, certain intriguing events during his journey had made his life fairly interesting and rewarding! For nearly thirty-eight of those years, his life had largely revolved around his profession as a police officer, where he had performed decently, although he never considered himself the quintessential insider.

On the eve of his golden sunset from a profession he loved, Avinash looked back at his life, right from his childhood to the present, with a degree of contentment. He knew he had lived his life, both professional and personal, with a sense of dignity and integrity.

Altogether, Avinash had the good fortune of being born and spending his childhood in the beautiful landscape in the heart of the Western Ghats, in a small community with quaint, but fast-changing traditions and belief systems. Thereafter, he had moved to the big cities of South and North India, in pursuit of higher education. Finally, his professional journey had taken him in turns to the Indo-Gangetic plains, the Himalayas and the capital city. Hence, he considered himself fortunate enough to have traversed the length and breadth of this beautiful and diverse land and understood some of its essence. As a police officer, he had also had the rare privilege of experiencing multifarious facets of policing; at times very different from each other, which greatly contributed to his learning. Then, there was the charm of life in small towns with their own unique flavours, different geographical settings, and their fair share of local mysteries! Avinash often remembered certain peculiar events, which had occurred during his professional and personal life, which he had never shared with anyone else.

He sometimes told himself, "There are some rather strange stories to be told about some of these places, someday!" But one thing he was clear about - the stories couldn't be about events where he was the hero. Who would read such boring stories, he had often wondered, especially when, in his own estimation, the sum total of his life's achievements were nothing much to speak of!

However, there were many events in his life, right from his early days to well into the end of his professional career, which were rather curious and sometimes altogether inexplicable! Why not narrate these stories to those interested in listening to it, Avinash pondered. After he had hung up his boots as a cop, he finally decided that he would tell at least a dozen such stories, if not all, recounting them as they happened. Stories of strange experiences, of fallibility, of failures, of deaths, of hope, and of beauty... but all wrapped under circumstances that were mysterious and defied common sense and logic. Stories of rather extraordinary encounters!

The Shrieks in the Woods

Nobody in Rajanagar town knew about Kamala's whereabouts anymore. Avinash had often wondered if Kamala was even alive anymore. It had been a long time since she had completely disappeared from her home, without any trace. Kamala would perhaps be over seventy years old, were she alive today. He also sometimes thought of Kamala's mother Parvathi Devi, who had been his math tutor for a short while, when he was in class five.

It all happened sometime in the early 70s, when Avinash was around nine years old. His family had moved from the beautiful village of Bettagrama in the Western Ghats to the small town of Rajanagar in the state of Karnataka. The main consideration behind this move was the education of Avinash and his siblings. There was a missionary school in Rajanagar and his parents thought that an English medium education would do the children some good; but Avinash dearly missed his beautiful village, Bettagrama.

In fact, Avinash had always been the happiest in Bettagrama. All through his early life, he had woken up every morning in Bettagrama to the melody of bird songs, so typical of a Western Ghats village. He had roamed the forests, the paddy fields and the coffee groves the whole day, without a care in the world. He had foraged for wild greens in the forest, gathered edible ferns from little stream beds, picked wild mushrooms from the carpet of fallen leaves and given them to his grandmother. Avinash was particularly fond of the small forest shrines that dotted Bettagrama; there were some in the form of small undefined figurines, some as ancient stones, some as old trees and others as graves of venerable ancestors. He used to shower wildflowers on the forest shrines whenever he passed them and prayed fervently that his village may remain unchanged forever!

Then there were the stories in the night by the domestic helps! The stories were mostly of fierce spirits who stalked the forests and hills, waiting to pounce upon unwary night travellers! Such stories acquired an even more sinister hue in the flickering light of the ancient brass lamps, since Bettagrama had no electricity back then. And yet he loved those stories, though he was too petrified to venture out of his old house after dark because of them!

But alas, Bettagrama did not have a good school nearby, and his parents were keen to give the children a decent education. They had all decided to move over to Rajanagar town.

Avinash liked Rajanagar town, too. It was unspoiled, had vigorous mountain air and a pleasant sleepiness, which can only be felt and cannot be described. The houses in the town were all well-spaced-out, and there was a quaint marketplace in the centre of the town which catered to everyone's needs. All the residents knew each other and lived harmoniously. The pleasant quality of the town was accentuated by the view of the distant blue mountains of the Western Ghats all around.

Avinash's daily routine in Rajanagar consisted of first waking up early in the morning to fetch milk from the market. It was a walk of around thirty minutes from the house one way, and he enjoyed the early morning mist and the crisp breeze, except during the monsoons, when it poured buckets for four months! But monsoons were nice, as he felt one with the elements. He would leave for school at around nine in the morning, again a walk of around thirty minutes, and after futile struggles with studies till four in the evening, it was finally a rush back to the house to await the best part of the day.

Around one kilometre from his house was a government school with a large playground. The school was almost on the edge of the town, with little or no habitation around. In the evening, it was time to rush post-haste there, to join the games with his friends. The games varied according to the seasons – it was mostly hockey or sometimes cricket during the summers. Also, kho-kho and kabbadi, when their equipment for the other two games suffered collective damage, which was quite often. During the monsoons, when all the outdoor games stopped, his destination was the small hostel of the government school, which had a table tennis facility donated by a kindly benefactor. His games routine would be over by around six. Thereafter, he was back to the house, to wash up and daydream in front of the books, pretending to be doing his homework.

In Rajanagar, the days were long, the heart was light and there was always a beautiful song in the air. The entire town was sound asleep by nine. Jackal packs howled in the night; their ululations having a comforting faraway quality to them.

The government school held a special fascination for Avinash for another reason as well. It was almost on the edge of a thickly wooded forest. It had towering tropical rainforest trees with thick canopies. Sunlight barely penetrated down to the forest floor. In the monsoons, the trees were thick with orchids and ferns, giving the trees a strange and colourful bearded appearance.

These woods were very dark at all times of the year. The playground and the small, lonely hostel of the government school almost abutted into the woods. According to local superstitions, the woods were the realm of the Goraga, a fierce male spirit, who did not take kindly to anybody intruding into his forest. Everyone from the town, including the children and grown-ups, gave a wide berth to this patch of the forest. Strangely, even the cattle avoided this place in spite of the abundant forage. While playing hockey or cricket in the nearby field, if the ball fell into the woods, it was abandoned by Avinash and his friends, since none of them could muster the courage to retrieve the ball. The boys residing in the hostel often related hair-raising stories of blood-curdling screams emanating from the woods, especially on moonless nights! It was purportedly a strident, piercing shriek, distinctly male in timbre, resonating through the forests. It was apparently the Goraga patrolling his woods! The boys in the hostel lived in abject terror of the Goraga.

Quite early on in their stay in the town, Avinash had become aware of the fact that there were definitely strange and inexplicable happenings in the Goraga forest. He had learnt of people who had developed mysterious fevers after accidentally straying into the woods. The woods abounded with various berries, wild fruits and other forest produce like honey, but no one in Rajanagar submitted bids for the government auction of the forest produce from these woods. The last bidder, it was believed, had lost his mind after he entered the forest for a collection of honey. Sometimes when Avinash watched the forest from the playground, the tree canopies swayed as if in a Mexican wave, even when there was no breeze! He also saw unexplained whirlwinds on the forest floor! There were many local stories of timber thieves entering the woods and getting slapped on their backs by an unseen entity. The shock was apparently so great that they would not speak for days! The fear of the Goraga woods was real and added a special quality of excitement to Avinash's life in Rajanagar town.

Towards the middle of Avinash's class five sojourn, it was discovered that his knowledge of math was almost negligible. His mother took matters into her own hands to stave off a major family crisis. He was to go for math tuitions.

A newly arrived math teacher in the government school, Parvathi Devi, agreed to be his tutor. She had taken up residence near the government school in a house not too far from the boys' hostel. In fact, it was the only house in the vicinity of the school. It was just a five-minute walk to the school for Parvathi Devi, hence very convenient. For some reason, the house had remained unoccupied for a long time after the previous residents had vacated it. But it was just the right house for Parvathi Devi: cosy, comfortable and spacious.

Parvathi Devi had been recently transferred from the plains to the Western Ghats. Perhaps it was government policy that all teachers should do a stint in the ghats. People from the plains usually found it difficult to adjust to the life in the hills. The lifestyle, culture, food preferences and the language were all different. Weather was also a factor – winters were cold, and the monsoons posed a major challenge for outsiders; it poured non-stop for months with howling winds.

Parvathi Devi was a widow with a grown-up daughter Kamala, who was then around twenty-four years old. Kamala was tall, graceful and very pleasant to look at. She had completed her graduation and was apparently waiting to get married. She had an insatiable appetite for reading what Avinash could vaguely discern as romantic novels. Both the mother and the daughter found it difficult to adjust to life in Rajanagar town initially and hardly had any interaction with the locals.

Parvathi Devi was also very orthodox in her ways. She was very finicky about the food she ate, the water she drank, and the utensils she used. She led a very simple and frugal life. Sometimes Avinash thought that Kamala chafed at her mother's ways, but would not say anything. Kamala was vivacious by nature and was curious to interact with the inhabitants of Rajanagar. She even managed to make acquaintance with one or two girls in the town and regularly exchanged romantic novels with them. She had a lovely voice and could beautifully render songs in the Carnatic style. It appeared very difficult for her to sit at home the whole day and do nothing. Perhaps Parvathi Devi's only goal was to get Kamala married to a good boy of the same community, and hence she was very particular that Kamala should not mix too much with anybody. She actively discouraged Kamala from seeking out friends from among the locals. Kamala was very stoic in accepting her situation, since in reality, her life also seemed to revolve completely around her mother.

Parvathi Devi was a fine math teacher, and very soon, Avinash's dread of numbers reduced. Her technique of teaching math was very different from other teachers. She used storytelling methods as a means to make mathematical propositions look very easy and his grasp of the subject improved in a very short time. It was very convenient for him to go to her house for the one-hour tuition, after his games routine at around 7 p.m. Kamala was always very kind to him and would ply him with delicious snacks every day, but always in utensils specially earmarked for him! It was usually quite dark when Avinash left for home after the tuition. The roads would be empty and the houses were few and far in between. He would break into a nervous non-stop run for home to avoid the imaginary Goraga chasing him! His only friend on the way was the single street light somewhat midway, which would always cast a kindly glow.

Avinash subsequently found that the routine day-to-day chores were not easy for Parvathi Devi and Kamala. They had to draw water for their daily use from an old well, a fair distance from the house on the edge of the woods. Then, firewood had to be split into the right portions for the wood-fired stove. Provisions had to be purchased from the market, which was a long walk away. For some reason, domestic helps refused to work in their house. Perhaps they found it difficult to adjust to Parvathi Devi's orthodox ways. It was at this point of time, maybe around a month after Avinash's tuition classes had started, that Rudra suddenly appeared on the scene and offered his services to help them. He claimed that he used to work for the previous tenants of the house as well. He said he was from the interior village of Cheyya, which was located beyond the Goraga woods.

Rudra instantly invoked fear in Avinash's young mind. He was extremely tall, muscular and strapping, with a fierce look about him. He had a big moustache with a long scar on his right cheek. He exuded an aura of silent menace. He was perhaps in his late thirties. Rudra always wore a spotless white lungi and white shirt and was scrupulously clean. His physical personality exuded an intimidating aura, especially when he looked at anyone with those piercing black eyes. His demeanour was anything but that of a domestic help! But he was a god-send for Parvathi Devi and Kamala. Now, drawing water from the well, splitting firewood and getting provisions, etc., were not a problem anymore. Rudra quietly did his work and seldom spoke or showed any extra interest in collecting his wages, which suited them fine.

There was one strange quality about Rudra. He would only emerge for housework at dusk, since he claimed that he had to look after his farm in the day time. He always walked from the direction of the Goraga woods, saying it was a shortcut from his village. He was perhaps the only person in the town who walked in the woods fearlessly without a concern in the world! He would collect firewood and jungle fruits and berries from the woods on his way, which were greatly relished by Kamala. He almost never spoke. He would finish his chores and walk back to his village through the woods nonchalantly!

One day, Avinash, out of curiosity, somehow mustered sufficient courage to quietly follow Rudra to the edge of the Goraga woods on his way back from work. As soon as Rudra entered the woods, he suddenly turned back to look at Avinash, eyes blazing! Avinash ran back in sheer terror, heart pounding and legs flailing with intense fear.

Avinash could see how Parvathi Devi and Kamala had become totally dependent on Rudra for running their household. Even the little interaction they had with the locals had reduced. Moreover, Rudra was resentful of anyone visiting their house, including Parvathi Devi's relatives from her native place. He also did not like Avinash much, which the latter could sense clearly. After Avinash's tuition classes were over, Rudra would sometimes silently follow him for some distance with a strange glint in his eyes. Avinash used to race home faster than usual, wanting to scream. Rudra also had this odd quality of not turning up for work on certain days of the month without any explanation.

At some point in time, Avinash noticed a distinct change in Kamala's behaviour. She had a strange spark in her eyes when Rudra was around. While earlier, she was relaxed and vivacious, now she was withdrawn, with a permanently preoccupied look. She always seemed extra eager to please Rudra. One day, Avinash saw Rudra and Kamala standing very close to each other in a dark corner outside Parvathi Devi's house. Things soon came to such a pass that over time, Kamala also seemed to have developed that silent, brooding quality that Rudra possessed. She hardly ate anything and developed an anaemic look, as if blood had drained from her face. But Parvathi Devi appeared totally oblivious to all these developments.

Time flew and soon Avinash's final exams were over. He had done decently well in mathematics! He went to Parvathi Devi's house to thank her for everything. Once there, he was greeted by the sight of Rudra in a towering rage. The reason that Avinash could gather was that Parvathi Devi was planning to go out of Rajanagar town during the summer holidays. Also, she had requested for a transfer out of Rajanagar to her hometown in the plains, citing difficulties in adjusting to life in the ghats, being a widow with a daughter of marriageable age. Rudra was livid with rage that Parvathi Devi had not consulted him before taking this step. As Avinash watched, Parvathi Devi was castigating Rudra in no uncertain terms that he was just a domestic help and she could do exactly what she felt like in her personal matters. She also ticked off Rudra and told him that his services were no longer required, given his impudence and unwarranted interference in their lives. A strange look came over Rudra as she said this and he suddenly stopped raging and looked at Parvathi Devi in a sneering manner. He left in a huff, saying, 'You brought it upon yourself.' Kamala was a silent bystander during this entire exchange, looking even more drained of blood than ever. That was the last anyone saw of Rudra in Rajanagar town.

In a few days, Parvathi Devi's transfer order came through. She was very happy and quickly completed the formalities of packing her belongings. However, just a day prior to her planned departure from Rajanagar town, Kamala suddenly disappeared in the evening hours! The only eyewitness to her disappearance was a little boy in the government hostel who said that he had seen Kamala walking towards the woods all alone in the evening at around 8 p.m.

Parvathi Devi filed a police complaint alleging that Rudra was most probably behind Kamala's disappearance and cited his parting words to her. The Rajanagar police launched a search in the Goraga woods for Kamala after mustering sufficient courage by enlisting a very large number of police personnel. A pair of slippers belonging to Kamala were recovered by them from deep in the forest. There was no trace of Kamala at all. The police went to Cheyya village to look for Rudra, but found that no person of that name or matching Rudra's description had ever lived there! Enquiries in the surrounding villages also yielded no results. No one in Rajanagar town had any information about Rudra. For all practical purposes, Rudra did not exist at all!

Parvathi Devi postponed her departure and waited in Rajanagar town for months together, hoping for some news of her only child. But the police were clueless. Parvathi Devi soon left Rajanagar for her hometown, distraught and heartbroken. Kamala's mysterious disappearance was a major event in the town and everyone had a theory of how and why Kamala had disappeared, but no one had any clear answers. The general excitement in Rajanagar town about Kamala's disappearance gradually petered out and life soon returned to an even keel as before. The police did not make any headway in Kamals's case and closed the matter after a few months.

Soon the monsoon rains broke over Rajanagar town. All the outdoor games stopped for Avinash. It was again table tennis in the evenings in the boys' hostel. This time around, the boys in the hostel were agog with chilling new tales of the woods! In the past, they had always heard a strident male shriek emanating from the forest. Of late, it was being answered by an equally strident female shriek! The boys were in a state of abject terror, especially in the nights during the dark phase of the moon, when the male and female shrieks were in tandem and seemingly had a triumphant note to them!

But who listens to the tales of small boys? The town people did not take them too seriously.

Kamala was never found. Even today, more than fifty years later, no one lives in the house Parvathi Devi had stayed in, which is now crumbling. The Goraga woods, if anything, have grown even denser. Many a time, Avinash – who subsequently went on to become a cop – often wondered who exactly was Rudra and why he was never found. Even in the police records, he could not find any evidence of Rudra's existence in Rajanagar town or in the surrounding villages!

Of late, Avinash has not checked with the boys in the small, lonely hostel if they still hear those dreadful male and female shrieks in tandem, especially on moonless nights!

Babu's Hurricane Lamp

For Avinash, his sisters and their cousins, a haircut by Babu, the village barber, was in many ways akin to a rite of passage. It was an ordeal they had to undergo every summer holidays in Bettagrama village during their childhood. The end result was a crew cut, regardless of the gender, with multiple nicks and cuts as badges of honour from the ancient pair of scissors and the razors of more or less the same vintage. It was their grandfather's rule that all the children in the household should get their hair cut from Babu during the annual school break following the family tradition. Babu was not just the village barber, but also a close family confidant.

Avinash did not know how Babu felt about the professional arrangements he had with Avinash's family, but it was assumed that the latter was very happy about it. It worked something like this – every year, after the paddy crop was harvested by his family, a decent measure of rice was earmarked for Babu, which was his annual fee. The contract required Babu to attend to Avinash's family whenever there were summons to cut someone's hair. In addition, in the village scheme of things, Babu was also required to be the conveyor of messages from Avinash's family to various relatives scattered around the district; the postal system being rudimentary and very slow during those days. Babu's mode of transport for such missions was usually by foot. In the 1970s, bus services in Bettagrama were scanty, and personal transport was almost unheard of. In fact it was Babu who had knocked at his town home at Rajanagar one early morning, when Avinash was around nine years old, to convey the sad news that his grandfather had passed away. Babu had walked all the way in the night from Bettagrama to Rajanagar, a distance of around fifteen kilometres, to convey the news. Babu had always been a part of his family, in grief and in happiness.

But after the death of Avinash's grandfather, the old order changed, the existing arrangements transformed and the previous economic ties altered. Babu realized the benefits of proper commercial relations with clients and opened a salon in the nearby town of Suryanagar, the only salon in that town at that time. Babu also educated his children well. His two sons and a daughter soon landed government jobs, which was a matter of great pride for him. But even after Avinash's grandfather's demise, Babu's relationship with Avinash's family continued to remain warm and affectionate.

Every year during the summer holidays, when Avinash visited Bettagrama, Babu was among the first visitors to come calling. He would invariably bring some homegrown vegetables and fruits as special gifts. He would even threaten Avinash and his cousins with an offer of a haircut, which was politely declined. Babu was a repository of all the village gossip and updated Avinash's family regularly on the happenings in Bettagrama village. Actually, nothing untoward ever happened in Bettagrama, except for someone's crop being destroyed by elephants or wild boars, or somebody's farm-help being lured away by another farm owner. Such was the nature of gossip Babu diligently collected for onward transmission! But he was a good man and very content with life, since his children had done well.

Over the years, his salon in Suryanagar suffered a general decline, as more fashionable outlets had cropped up all over. However, he had some traditional die-hard clients who kept the establishment going. Plus, Babu was the go-to man whenever there was any death in and around Suryanagar town and the family members concerned were required to ritually shave their hair.

Avinash soon entered college in Chennai in the early 1980s, having done decently in his school exams. As a result, his visits to Bettagrama were reduced to just twice a year – once during the December break and then during the summer holidays. Actually, once he and his siblings entered college, his parents had moved back to their ancestral village of Bettagrama from their temporary residence at Rajanagar town. Babu always squeezed in time during Avinash's visits to Bettagrama and would update the latter with all the latest developments in the village. While many of his contemporaries in the village had passed away, Babu was healthy and continued to work his small patch of land, apart from his hair-cutting duties. His children sent him money regularly, and he had built a decent house in Bettagrama village, which was his pride and joy.

Avinash usually reached Bettagrama late at night from Chennai during the college breaks. He would first catch the mid-day train from Chennai to Bangalore, reaching in the evening. Thereafter, he immediately took the first available bus from Bangalore to Suryanagar, a distance of around 250 kms. He reached Suryanagar by around 11 p.m. and walked the remaining 6 kms to Bettagrama, only to arrive home by midnight or a little later. In the early 1980s, there were no night cabs or auto services in Suryanagar town and the passengers who alighted from late night bus services invariably walked to their respective destinations.

Avinash always found the night walk from Suryanagar town to Bettagrama village very interesting. Suryanagar was a small town with a population of only around a thousand people, and after a few minutes of walk, one crossed the town limits and entered deserted village roads. There were no streetlights along the way. On both sides of the road to Bettagrama village, there were coffee groves with tall shade trees. At places, the pattern was broken by wide expanses of rice fields. The homesteads were few and far in between, which was very typical of this part of the Western Ghats. On moonlit nights, it was a beautiful walk, although a lonely one, without a single person in sight during the entire journey! On moonless nights, it was a challenging journey, and one had to be careful of poisonous snakes, especially after rain when the frogs came out. Then, around mid-way en route, there was the burial ground. It was actually an old burial ground which had been abandoned a long time ago; but the old and bleached tomb-stones stood in stark contrast to the surrounding background. Despite the darkness, they were clearly visible to Avinash in the moonlight or even in starlight and the atmosphere was always rather eerie. On dark nights, the graveyard appeared deathly still! Although Avinash had walked this route countless times, the burial ground always made him slightly uneasy and breathe a little faster! Usually, all along the route to Bettagrama village from Suryanagar town, there was the gentle sound of rustling of leaves of coffee shade trees, but around the graveyard, it abruptly stopped! That said, in all his years, Avinash had reached Bettagrama without any mishap or even a single sighting of any other-worldly apparitions.

This time around, Avinash had reached Suryanagar at around 11 p.m. on a misty and rather windy December night. To his pleasant surprise, he found Babu in the process of closing his shop. Together, they set out towards Bettagrama. Babu informed him that he had been delayed since there was a death in a village near Suryanagar town and he had to attend to the rituals of the family concerned. Avinash was also relieved that he had company for his journey home on such a misty night. Avinash found Babu in a very happy state of mind. Babu informed Avinash that he had recently become a grandfather.

Soon, both of them crossed Suryanagar town, and the mist became much more intense on the way, as if strings of low clouds were hovering all around. The wind was also blowing with almost the force of a gale. Fortunately, Babu was carrying an old hurricane lamp with him and they both found their way to Bettagrama without too much difficulty. The lamp appeared to be ancient, but was very well maintained. The brass was well polished and the wick neatly trimmed. Despite the strong wind, the lamp never fluttered and provided a steady stream of light for the journey. Babu told Avinash that he had always used this hurricane lamp during his night journeys from Suryanagar town to Bettagrama. Babu also enquired about Avinash's studies and other activities and was pleased to know that Avinash wanted to try to get into the police service after his graduation.

As they were crossing the burial ground, Avinash got talking to Babu about his slight dread whenever he crossed the place and how he found that all of a sudden, it became deathly still near the graveyard! But Babu had a very simple explanation to offer for the stillness. He explained to Avinash that all along the route, there were coffee shade trees which rustled at the slightest breeze, but the graveyard was in the open ground and without trees, hence the rustling abruptly stopped. Babu further told Avinash that ghosts and spirits do not exist in the real world and are only conjured out of the imaginations of fearful minds. Both of them soon entered Bettagrama village and since Babu's house was around half a kilometre before Avinash's, he turned left, bade goodbye and handed over the hurricane lamp to Avinash for the onward journey.

A few minutes later, Avinash reached home, extinguished the lamp, kept it on the veranda, and knocked at the door. He was home at last!

Next morning, when he woke up, he did not find the hurricane lamp and asked his mother about it. Avinash told her that it had to be returned to Babu since he had borrowed it from him the previous night.

Avinash's mother appeared very annoyed and scolded him, saying, "You are always playing the fool! You must have come to know that Babu died in his shop last week. It is in very bad taste to mock the death of an old family confidant in this manner!"

Avinash kept quiet, and in spite of searching everywhere, could not find Babu's old hurricane lamp anywhere!

A couple of years later, Avinash actually got into the police service and he sometimes fondly remembered Babu for the similarity of his childhood haircuts with the ones they gave him at the police academy!

Ghanvat Uikey

Sonepur was an ancient land, part of the Gondwana belt – a fascinating place with many sites of palaeolithic and microlithic remains. Sonepur also abounded in pre-historic fossil locations of algae and stromatolites, which provided information about life in the planet in the bygone ages! It was a serendipitous accident of government service that Avinash, early on in his career as a police officer, was posted there as the Superintendent of Police. Prior to this posting, Avinash had served as an understudy in a couple of districts in the timeless land of the Ganga and the Yamuna, after he had completed his training at the police academy.

Sonepur was also the old tiger country during the British times. There was the legendary story of a district collector of those times, who served in Sonepur for fourteen years and used to disappear into deep forests whenever a messenger from the headquarters arrived with his transfer order! The transfer orders apparently could never be served to him and the collector endlessly indulged in his favourite sport of shikar. By the time Avinash got his posting to Sonepur in the early

1990s, the tigers were all long gone; hunted or extinct locally due to habitat destruction. However, Sonepur still had fairly thick, disjointed pockets of forests. During the monsoons, the place was a visual delight with green undulating hills and myriad waterfalls. The river Sona flew through the district with crystal clear waters and golden sand banks. Avinash loved lush landscapes and was the happiest in such pleasing natural settings.

Avinash's wife Amrita and son Nitin also immediately liked the feel of Sonepur; a far cry from the dust and din of the normal district towns. They sometimes went for long drives in the night through the forested parts of Sonepur in the hope of sighting some wildlife. Little Nitin, who was only four years old, immensely liked the vast outdoors, especially the picnics on the banks of river Sona with families of other officers. And then there was the cable TV, which had just made an entry into the country! Avinash and Amrita were avid watchers of such silly serials like *Santa Barbara* and *The Bold and The Beautiful!*

Avinash's new assignment in Sonepur was also a welcome change for him, as the previous assignment was in a communally charged place with recurring high-stress events. Sonepur was situated in a remote corner of the state, with few apparent policing problems. The only cause for concern was the incipient Naxal situation. Sonepur was located at the tri-junction of three states in the Chota Nagpur Plateau, and the Naxal problem in the other two states was acute. There was always the fear of a spill over of the problem from the other states. Sonepur was located in the adivasi heartland of India populated by Gonds, Aghariyas, Baigas, Kharwars, et al. Memorably, on the very first night of his arrival at Sonepur, it was peerless for him to hear the distant throb of tribal drum beats and songs.

But Sonepur was a place of contrasts – the remote tribal settlements were interspersed with spanking new townships, mostly thermal power projects and other industrial undertakings. These projects displaced many tribal settlements and their way of life. But the compensation packages were fairly generous. The displaced families had better access to modern amenities and education. They were also economically better off than their brethren in the interior villages. And yet, they seemed to have lost their cultural moorings in the strange new urban settings. There were certain elements in Sonepur and outside, who stoked such latent fires, for the sake of an ideology with a premium on violence, rather than assisting the population to transition into their new and more comfortable settings while retaining their distinct identity and culture.

Avinash could sense that given the remoteness and lack of connectivity of most parts of Sonepur, the social tensions of displacement and the growing Naxal presence in the neighbouring states, it was a ready cocktail for potential policing challenges. It warranted that the police formulate a proper plan to urgently address these issues before matters went out of hand.

Avinash devised a two-pronged strategy, which broadly consisted of police outreach towards the adivasi communities and strict enforcement of laws. As to the latter part, Sonepur had an anachronistic legacy from the British times. The local population, at some time in history, had been allowed to keep muzzle-loading guns and rifles without licenses, ostensibly for crop protection. But even after the passage of the Disarming Act subsequently, many of them continued to hold arms, without licenses. Avinash surmised that potentially – given these ancient but functional weapons and the perfect knowledge of their terrain – there could be serious problems if the Naxal influence grew in the countryside. So, he decided that the police would crack down and confiscate these weapons. At the same time, he decided that the police would hold extensive meetings in remote outposts with the tribal communities to hear their grievances, redress them, and also educate them on the violence and sufferings that Naxalism unleashes. Avinash also started training a team of young police personnel in jungle warfare tactics to meet any eventuality in the future.

It was during one of these outreach programmes that Avinash first met Ghanvat Uikey. He was a Gond, perhaps in his early thirties, and a self-proclaimed tribal activist. The meeting was in the remote police station of Rone, close to the interstate borders. Ghanvat Uikey was dressed in a suit and tie in a predominantly tribal gathering and his sartorial preference was rather incongruous in such a setting! He also seemed well-educated and spoke his mind fearlessly. Apparently, his education had been facilitated by a local NGO. He proudly informed the audience that he was a graduate in philosophy and had opted to live in the village of his birth to serve the adivasi community. He also recounted the glorious history of the adivasi communities of the country and narrated how, due to the alleged indifference of the government machinery, the adivasis had been exploited, impoverished and pushed into the margins of the society. Everybody in the audience listened intently to Ghanvat, including the policemen, who had certain preconceived notions about the adivasi way of life. Ghanvat strongly raised the issue of the police department confiscating muzzleloaders and prosecuting the owners. He contended that these weapons had not been used for generations and a very large number of households possessed them. He argued that if the district police cracked down on these ancient weapons at so many tribal homes, it would completely alienate them and drive them into the lap of the Naxals. He assured that people would voluntarily deposit such weapons at the police stations, for they had no use for them. He wanted a guarantee that the gun owners will not be prosecuted for possession of unlicensed weapons. The argument sounded reasonable to Avinash and he agreed. The police thereafter changed their strategy, stopped the crackdown and started requesting people to deposit their unlicensed weapons at the police stations in the entire district. Most people complied. The police also organized bails for those who had been unfortunately prosecuted earlier. In this manner, most of Sonepur was disarmed without the attendant social costs. This cemented Avinash's friendship with Ghanvat Uikey.

Ghanvat was an inveterate crusader on a number of real and sometimes imaginary tribal issues. Mostly, he would take up the cases of harassment of adivasis by the government machinery, especially the forest department. He had limited income and resources at his disposal – a small agriculture patch that catered to his family's basic requirements and a clutch of chicken and goats, which he used to sell in the nearby town, where there was a good demand for these products. He used to make at least two trips a month to the district headquarters from his remote village of Garadiya, always dressed in his trademark suit and tie, and submit petitions to the district authorities. He spent considerable money, time and energy on these pursuits. He had to walk through the forest path from Garadiya to Rone, a good fifteen kms away, cross the Rone river in a country-made boat, and take whatever irregular local bus service that was available, to the district headquarters from Rone. His dream project was the construction of a bridge over the Rone river, a road connecting the bridge to Garadiya, and the opening of a primary school in his village. He worked tirelessly on getting these projects going, with touching faith in the official machinery, which perhaps had many other priorities. He always paid Avinash a visit when he came to the district headquarters and they chatted about various issues over a cup of tea.

Ghanvat's views on the future of the adivasi communities in the country were very different from those of the many activists in Sonepur, who professed to espouse their cause. Ghanvat was rather contemptuous of the non-tribal activists, who he believed, overly romanticised the adivasi way of life and advocated isolationism. He was firmly of the view that a lifestyle based on the old adivasi practices of living off the earth with subsistent economic practices was not viable anymore. While he dearly loved the Gondi lifestyle and cultural practices, he felt that no culture could flourish if mere day-to-day existence became a challenge. He had clear views that the adivasi villages needed connectivity, schools and medical facilities.

At the same time, Ghanvat was passionate that the government should patronize adivasi art and culture, so that it is institutionally preserved for posterity. Even in his own village, he found many ancient Gondi lifestyle traditions dying out. Ghanvat's views of his own community irked many activists of Sonepur, who believed that the tribal way of life was in complete harmony with the environment and the state should withdraw from all those activities, which they believed disrupted such an environment. So, Ghanvat was at crosshairs with many activists because of his contrary views. They often had passionate debates on tribal issues in the local newspapers.

On a beautiful October morning, around two years after he had first met Ghanvat, Avinash received information from the Rone police station that a large group of armed Naxals had entered Garadiya village, probably from the neighbouring state. This information was conveyed to the police station by Mangru Markem, the Garadiya village chowkidar, who had sneaked out of the village upon noticing the armed Naxal group. Avinash decided to immediately proceed to Garadiya with a team of specially trained police officials to deal with the situation. They drove till Rone and crossed the river in a country boat which ferried passengers to and fro. Thereafter, it was a march of around fifteen kilometres through undulating terrain. They were quite fortunate to have Mangru Markem with them, since he knew the terrain well.

Even after so many years, Avinash still remembers that march to Garadiya through the pristine Sal forests of unmatched beauty. There was also a proliferation of bamboo growth all along the innumerable rivulets with crystal clear water. The police party was constantly on the alert for a possible ambush by the Naxals and avoided the beaten track. However, when they were still five kilometres away from Garadiya, it became dark and Avinash decided to halt the march. He was acutely aware that the Naxals could take advantage of the dark and launch an attack on the police party. They chose a large rocky outcrop in the jungle to halt for the night. It was on the ridge of a hillock and commanded a good view of the surrounding area on all sides. Avinash decided that the police party would resume its march to Garadiya just before first light the next morning.

As Avinash and his colleagues ate their meagre rations, a beautiful silver moon rose over the Sal forests. He posted four sentries in the four directions of the rocky outcrop and soon dozed off, lulled by the cool forest breeze. He did not know for how long he had slept, but suddenly, he felt as if he was being jolted violently by someone. When Avinash opened his eyes, he thought he saw a shadowy figure of a man in a suit and tie looking at him and silently pointing his fingers towards the west. As if in a dream, the man was gone in a blur. None of the sentries seemed to have noticed the shadowy presence. Avinash looked and listened intensely in the direction pointed out by the shadowy figure and he could discern the faintest rustle of dry leaves and the slightest hint of a movement. As quietly as possible, he alerted his team. The firing from both sides was almost simultaneous! But Avinash's party was prepared and had the advantage of higher ground. The firing on the other side stopped after around fifteen minutes. Somehow, the Naxals had come to know of their resting place and had planned a surprise attack. The police party had reacted in time and nobody in Avinash's team was hurt.

Early the next morning, the police searched the area and found copious amounts of blood at many Naxal positions, but did not find any dead bodies. It was likely that the Naxal group had removed the dead bodies and evacuated the injured under the cover of darkness. Avinash's team thereafter resumed its march to Garadiya village without any further delay. Soon, they reached their destination.

Garadiya was a typical Gond village, with neat rows of mud and thatch houses, which were scrupulously clean. The mud walls were painted with figures in vivid bright colours in the typical Gondi technique of lines and dots. Garadiya was a beautiful village, untouched by civilization. But on reaching Garadiya village, Avinash was shocked to discover that Ghanvat Uikey had been brutally killed by the Naxals the previous day.

Avinash and his team reached his house, only to find Ghanvat's dead body lying in front of his house. Ghanvat's wife Sukalo and his two small boys appeared too terrorized to even shed tears. Ghanvat's body had been brutalized beyond recognition. Both his legs and hands were broken with what appeared to be lathi blows. His throat was slit, and a large pool of blood had flown and congealed on the ground. A dignified human being, who fancied wearing idiosyncratic attire and took up tribal causes selflessly, was shorn of all dignity in death. Avinash found it difficult to hold back his tears. Why do human beings inflict such unspeakable atrocities on other human beings, that too for an outdated ideology, he wondered.

The story was short, as gathered from the villagers. A group of Naxals had arrived at Garadiya the previous day. They had singled out Ghanvat; perhaps they had prior information that he was in touch with the outside world, especially the district administration. They had held a sham Kangaroo court and 'tried' him on charges of being a 'police informer' and indulging in 'anti-tribal activities'. They had read out the sham evidence and called upon the villagers to provide contrary evidence, if any, in his favour. Nobody dared to, in the face of their automatic weapons. Thereafter, Ghanvat was beaten black and blue and executed by slitting his throat in front of the entire village, including his wife and children.

'Kill one to terrorize thousands', a classic tactic of all terrorists, Avinash remembered. The Naxals had left the village, threatening to come back if the police were informed of the murder. According to the villagers, the group appeared to be from across the state border and the leader was being referred to as 'Venkat' by the others. The only consolation for Avinash was the fact that the police had inflicted considerable damage on the Naxal group that had perpetrated this senseless killing.

It has been a long time since this incident happened. Now there is a bridge over the Rone river and a road that connects Garadiya to that bridge. But there is still no school which Ghanvat had dreamt of. Nevertheless, it all came a little too late for Ghanvat Uikey, the man who fiercely took up tribal causes.

As for Avinash, he firmly believes that Ghanvat saved his life in the most inexplicable manner, and will forever be indebted to him.

The Uncanny Experience in Behta Village

Although quite close to the state capital of a large state in the country, Haidalpur district was light years away from any trappings of modernity. The defining feature of the district was desolation. The land and water in the district were saline, and the landscape was dotted with coarse grass and the occasional stunted babool tree. Agriculture was limited and villages were few and far in between. Even the district headquarters conveyed the impression of a long-forgotten outpost. It was difficult to even get fresh provisions and vegetables there. The local people largely kept to themselves, induced perhaps by the dreariness of their surroundings, which dulled the normal senses.

Haidalpur was also the land of vendetta killings. Family feuds, mostly over scarce agricultural land, were kept alive for generations. The district recorded one of the highest incidences of homicides. Multiple killings due to old enmities were a common feature, but rarely created a sensation. The people had profound faith in settling their own scores, rather than relying on the intricacies of availing the benefits of the criminal justice system. Despite the high crime rate, Haidalpur was a surprisingly easy assignment for a police officer to manage, as most of the murders were solved since they arose out of ongoing disputes. The culprits were usually known. Also, unlike in most places, crimes rarely led to public order problems, since the populace was largely inured to violence. Hence, for a police officer, the work was largely routine, comprising visits to the crime scenes, monitoring arrests of the accused, and finally, prosecuting them. Travelling for long hours through the dreary landscape for this purpose added to the monotony and a general sense of desolation in the atmosphere.

It was on a July morning sometime in the middle of the 1990s that Avinash received the message of a suspected double murder of an unidentified young couple in village Behta under the Sarangarh police station limits. Avinash was posted as the police chief of Haidalpur, and Sarangarh was the remotest part of the district with sparse inhabitation. Here, the soil salinity was at its highest and the entire topography had a bleached look, with almost no agriculture or any other redeeming physical features.

Avinash had already spent nearly a year in Haidalpur before this incident and was considered a competent officer, especially in controlling crime. In addition to vendetta murders, Haidalpur was also known for gangs of marauding bandits in some of its remote locations falling in the ravines. The bandit gangs were generally formed on the basis of caste and carried out depredations against other castes, whom they considered inimical to them. So Avinash often had to conduct operations against such gangs after mobilizing police forces in large numbers. He liked such operations because the ravines offered an interesting geographical setting and were very different from the rest of Haidalpur.

While Haidalpur in general had very few redeeming features beyond routine work, for Avinash and his family, close friendships and bonds with other fellow officers were compensation for the near absence of modern amenities and avenues of entertainment.

On that July morning, Avinash arrived at Sarangarh police station after breakfast, intending to inspect the scene of crime of the suspected double murder. He was told by Man Singh, the station-in-charge, that the information of the incident had been conveyed to the police station in the wee hours of the morning by a young lad, Chatar Singh, who claimed to be the son of Buddhan, the village chowkidar of Behta. A case of murder had been registered on the basis of his information. The lad had also claimed that his father, Buddhan, was prevented from conveying this information to the police by Mandaleshwar, the sarpanch of Behta, and his henchmen, who had also allegedly severely assaulted Buddhan in the process. Chatar Singh also informed Man Singh that the family members of Buddhan were rushing Buddhan to the government hospital at Haidalpur for the treatment of his injuries and he himself was also proceeding there shortly.

Man Singh, the station-in-charge of Sarangarh, was an unusual police officer. He had a reputation for meticulously registering all crimes reported to his police station. While he would vigorously pursue the cases of heinous offenses and prosecute the accused, he would go to great lengths to mediate a compromise between the parties involved in minor crimes and petty disputes to their mutual satisfaction. He was very popular with the people of his jurisdiction, wherever he was posted, for this reason. Also, Man Singh was an upright police officer and known for his probity.

Man Singh also apprised Avinash of a rather strange and unusual fact about Behta village. Every police station maintains a record known as the village crime notebook, which is a register containing all important details of the villages under that particular police station's jurisdiction. Such details include the population composition of the village, the notable village functionaries, the record of year-wise crime in the village, the list of 'history sheeters' or bad characters, etc. In this register, Behta village was shown as an uninhabited village for over eighty years! No policeman had ever visited this village during this period and no crime had ever been reported! The last entry in the register mentioned that due to progressive soil and water salinity, village Behta had been abandoned a long time ago!

Avinash and the police party soon left for the scene of crime in a jeep, just as the monsoon rains were breaking over Sarangarh. The route to Behta village was through the small village of Bhogni as recorded in the village crime notebook. It was with considerable difficulty that they reached Bhogni, since the route was tortuous; the mud roads having been rendered into sticky morass due to the rains. Upon reaching Bhogni, they made enquiries about the location of Behta, but received no definitive answers from the villagers. Some old-timers gave them the general direction, with the rider that no one had visited Behta village for a long time, since it was believed to be abandoned. The police party found the route to Behta even more desolate and stark. There was an odd, other-worldly and lifeless feel to the landscape. The salt from the groundwater had risen to the surface at many places, giving the topography an unhealthy whitish pallor.

There was a complete absence of vegetation or animal life. The dark rain clouds made it look even more foreboding. After travelling for nearly an hour, the police party finally reached what Avinash presumed was Behta village. The village had a grim and desolate air about it. The most defining feature of the village was a single but strange-looking gnarled babool tree with tentacle-like branches. A normal village in this part of the world is usually a hive of activity with typical sounds and smells. But the main feature of this village was the utter silence and the total absence of any activity. The village had about twenty-five to thirty households with men and women standing in front of their homes and looking at Avinash and his team as if in a pantomime, with expressions of extreme resentment and hostility. Another feature of the village was the complete absence of children and young people and the positive energy it generates. The whole population appeared to be of somewhat the same, but indeterminate age! The entire village conveyed an impression of sullenness, hate, anger, despair and gloom. Avinash noticed that even Man Singh seemed to have felt this odd sensation, since he involuntarily shuddered.

The police were soon directed by a villager to the house where the two dead bodies were lying. The dead bodies were of a young couple in their late twenties. Both the corpses were almost lifelike in death, but with incredibly sorrowful expressions on their faces. The girl had streams of dried-up tears running down her cheeks. Their visages in death portrayed a feeling of utter hopelessness and despair. In fact, Avinash immediately felt that they seemed to have died of extreme anguish, if such a thing is possible!

The preliminary examination of the two dead bodies by the police did not disclose any apparent signs of injury on either of them. There were no outward manifestations of possible poisoning too. Strangulation was also ruled out since there were no telltale impressions on their necks. While Man Singh was completing the inquest proceedings as a precursor to referring the bodies for post-mortem, Avinash directed a policeman to call the village sarpanch to the spot. The sarpanch soon arrived and introduced himself as Mandaleshwar. He was accompanied by his henchman in tow, who went by the name of Mara. Both of them were burly individuals with a quality of defiance and anger in their demeanour. Avinash could sense that while usually the villagers in these parts were deferential to public authorities, these two men were haughty and irreverent with a quiet menace to their persona. The sarpanch was a silent man and had an odd way of looking over people with rolled-up eyeballs. The henchman was a rough, shifty-eyed individual, who upon questioning, informed Avinash that the deceased couple were not from the village. They had apparently arrived from somewhere suddenly, the previous night, and were staying in the vacant house where they were found dead in the morning. They had also not disclosed their identities to the villagers. He further claimed that nobody had killed them. At this point, the sarpanch interjected with a cryptic statement, 'They died because they could not live here.' All further efforts to elicit more information about the case failed since none of the other villagers would talk and the police were met with vacant stares to all the questions. Even normal questions regarding the village about their livelihood, source of drinking water, supply of essential items, etc., were replied to by Mara with a bland, 'We are self-sufficient and don't need anything from outside.' The duo also vehemently denied that they had assaulted the village chowkidar Buddhan in a bid to prevent him from informing the police about this incident.

Soon, rain started pouring steadily and Avinash and his team hastened to complete the formality of sealing the dead bodies and dispatching them for post-mortem to the Haidalpur hospital. Somehow, Avinash wanted to leave that dreadful place and not be stranded there for the night because of the rain. The police left with the intention of returning early the next morning for further investigation into the case. As regards the dead couple, Avinash arrived at a preliminary conclusion that most probably, they were a runaway couple in love, who had stumbled into Behta inadvertently. As to their probable cause of death, he decided to wait for the findings of the post-mortem. Avinash also made a mental note to speak to the village chowkidar Buddhan and his son Chatar Singh as soon as possible. He was hopeful that they'd still be present in Haidalpur hospital. The police party was greatly relieved to leave the gloomy village with its sullen and strange inhabitants.

On their way back, Avinash decided to make more inquiries in Bhogni about Behta village and its residents. The villagers of Bhogni again affirmed that Behta was a long-abandoned village, but one old man, Phagu Singh informed Avinash that his grandfather had fled Behta when he was a young man and had settled down in Bhogni village. He recounted to the police what his grandfather had told him about Behta.

A certain sarpanch, whose name Phagu could not recollect, had taken over as the headman of Behta. He demanded absolute loyalty from the villagers. He was extremely ruthless with those who defied his diktats or with those villagers who he thought would pose a challenge to his position in the future. In this endeavour, he was assisted by a henchman and the atrocities committed by the duo soon resulted in many villagers fleeing Behta. They were particularly resentful of people trying to educate themselves. The duo had grim personal tastes and preferences and had banned all celebrations and entertainment in the village. Most of the young people left the village since they found the regimentation of the two brothers intolerable. But the sarpanch also had many loyal supporters who were extremely faithful to him and reported upon others who were not. This would invite even more serious reprisals on such unfortunate villagers. The bad reputation of the village soon spread far and wide and no one would give their daughters in marriage to the boys of Behta village. As time passed by, the village became more and more insular and almost lost contact with the outside world. The paranoia in Behta had become so pronounced that outsiders who strayed into the village were treated with extreme hostility and threats of physical violence. At some point of time in history, all interaction of Behta villagers with the outside world snapped. This was the gist of the story that the police could piece together about Behta village from their conversation with Phagu Singh, as told to him by his own grandfather a long time ago.

Avinash and his team started early for Behta village the next morning. The rains had ceased, and it was easier to find their way since the jeep track of the previous day was faintly visible. Avinash was a little surprised that they had not reached Behta even after travelling for a considerable period. They scoured the area thoroughly to locate the village, but could only find a few gnarled babool trees with tentacle-like branches here and there, but no village! It was all very puzzling and inexplicable for the police party. Since there was no rational explanation for this, the police party intensified their search, but still could not trace the village at all. It was as if Behta village was lost in the immense vastness of the saline landscape! Also, the dreariness and the desolation of the area was starker and more dreadful compared to the previous day. Avinash was seized by a powerful feeling that he would never be able to leave that place! Others in the party also seemed to be going through similar emotions. Avinash finally decided to call off the search at around 4 p.m. and returned to the headquarters, deeply baffled by the turn of events.

The only remaining link in the chain was for the police to contact Chatar Singh or Buddhan, who should be present in Haidalpur government hospital. The police party reached there, but found no details in the hospital records of Buddhan having been admitted the previous day for the treatment of his alleged injuries! The government hospital was an old institution dating back to the late 1800s and its records were remarkably well-maintained. Avinash was curious to check if there was any reference to Behta village in its medico-legal records. After a great deal of scrutiny, he found a mention of Behta dating back to the year 1909! One Buddhan had been admitted to the hospital with severe assault injuries and had subsequently succumbed to his injuries. There were no further details of that case in the records.

Next, Avinash wanted to know the outcome of the post-mortem examination of the deceased couple. The probable cause of death of both of them was determined by the doctors as 'heart failure due to stress induced cardiomyopathy.' There were no ante-mortem injuries of any kind on their bodies. Avinash got talking to Dr Ashutosh Pande who had conducted the post-mortem and asked him how such a young couple, otherwise healthy-looking, could die of heart failure. The doctor also found it puzzling and informed that sometimes extreme and sudden emotional stress could result in a heart failure, which is also referred to as the 'broken heart syndrome'. Dr Pande informed that possibly, the girl had died slightly earlier. Avinash felt that the extreme emotional stress for the couple could only have been the total and complete loss of all hope and happiness of being trapped forever in that soulless village with its sullen inhabitants, bereft of all positive human emotions like love, empathy and compassion.

All further efforts by the police to identify the couple by displaying their photographs in newspapers, television, etc., elicited no response. Also, no one came forward to claim the dead bodies, which were kept in the government hospital morgue for a mandatory waiting period to see if there were any claimants. After the waiting period was over, the bodies were quietly cremated by the police and the ashes dispersed in a small river near Haidalpur. All subsequent efforts by the police to locate Behta village failed. However, over the years, there were stray accounts from the bandits of the ravines arrested by the police, of encountering a strange village during their depredations, which was beyond Bhogni and inhabited by peculiar inhabitants with no possessions!

The alleged murder case of the couple was finally closed by the police since the deaths were deemed as arising out of natural causes, given the post-mortem findings.

Today, if one were to read the Sarangarh police station records of this incident, it does not tell the entire story of the bizarre village which disappeared and Avinash's uncanny experience during the investigation of the death of the young couple. The police station entries also do not mention how young people may suddenly die out of extreme loss of hope and happiness! Man Singh, the police station-in-charge, was after all, a mere police officer and could not have made such profound metaphysical observations in the police station records!

And the Behta village remains listed as an uninhabited village in the records of Sarangarh police station to this day.

The Walks in the Park

Avinash worked in an investigation agency under the central government in the early 2000s. He enjoyed the work and the general ambience of the investigation agency's headquarters in the capital city, with its musty-smelling rooms full of case files and old documents. He knew that contrary to general perception, while crime investigation did involve a lot of leg work, ultimately it was how meticulously the records of a case were constructed that resulted in its successful prosecution. Over the years, he had dealt with a bewildering range of cases in the agency – murder cases, corruption cases, terrorism-related offences, bank frauds and several others. But his favourites were always the old, unsolved murder cases! There was a dingy section in his office that housed the case files of such old, unsolved crimes and he derived great pleasure in painstakingly going through those case files when he had free time. He enjoyed reading the statements of witnesses recorded a long time ago, poring over the crime scene photographs, studying the medical and forensic reports and reimagining the crime –

all over again! Sometimes, this exercise resulted in looking at those old cases from an entirely different perspective, yielding valuable insights to pursue new leads. There was a special thrill in revisiting those old scenes of crime, armed with a new perspective and a fresh set of questions for the witnesses and suspects. The thrill was even greater when occasionally Avinash could crack open a long-forgotten murder case and apprehend the accused when they least expected it! However, the long hours of such sedentary work warranted that Avinash should do regular fitness activities. He took to walking in the famous park near his office. The same big park where everyone walked; in the heart of the capital city, with ancient mausoleums, tall trees, a water body and petty egos!

In the beginning, Avinash was fairly oblivious to the atmosphere and vibrations of the famous park. It was just an uneventful brisk walk before he returned home. Then, one day, there was a massive storm and many trees in the park were uprooted. It was for the first time that Avinash thought he heard the sound of silent weeping in the park as he walked. He felt as if the trees that had survived were mourning their fallen comrades! It was a mystery to Avinash how the trees could transmit such emotions to him. Quite possibly, it was all his own imagination, but it was the beginning of his rather curious interaction with the trees in the park. That day, he had found it difficult to bear the seeming burden of their sorrow after the devastation caused by the storm. He felt that the mother of a fallen bottlebrush tree was particularly inconsolable. The youngster was only two years old; a bright future ahead with beautiful blooms every March to September had been tragically cut short. Avinash did what he could to console the survivors by touching them gently. The trees seemed to appreciate his concern. But ultimately, he realized that the trees were very resilient; they had seen it all before. Once he had gained their trust, he started believing that the trees slowly started unravelling the secrets of the park to him! The trees, for example, communicated to him in conspiratorial ways about the 'unseen people' who lived behind the locked gates and the blocked staircases of the ancient mausoleums! The 'unseen people' did not bother anybody and were very shy. Sometimes on foggy winter evenings, when there were a few walkers in the park, Avinash could see the 'unseen people' hesitantly coming out. If anyone approached them, they slowly walked farther and farther away and seemingly melted into the monuments again! They wore strange attires of times long gone by! He believed that the trees knew all about them and appeared to be their friends.

Avinash also felt that the trees knew everything about the people who walked on the paths in their shadows. They had their own apparent share of likes and dislikes. They liked good people and little children, but appeared to have a serious dislike for the pompous lot! The trees had a great sense of humour too, targeting an egoistic, bald braggart almost every day. Often, as the braggart walked along with his cronies, the trees would summon their friends, the birds, who deposited their droppings on his bald head! The braggart would momentarily stop bragging, wipe his head and start all over again! He was totally impervious to bird droppings on his bald head! The trees would shake with silent laughter whenever he walked under them. Some young trees also seemed to be fond of flirting with pretty girls and Avinash would often see a young Amaltas tree shower his petals on all the passing girls. The girls would look up momentarily startled and walk on with happy smiles on their faces!

It also appeared to Avinash as if the trees were scared of a certain category of people and felt very vulnerable before them. Sometimes, when such people walked in the park, Avinash could sense the trees telling their friends, the resident dogs of the park to harass them, hoping they would never walk in the park again! Once Avinash believed he understood the subterranean interaction between the trees, the 'unseen people', the birds, the dogs and the secret bond they all shared, his walks in the park became very interesting.

One of the regular walkers in the park was Brijesh Mahapal. He was a successful public figure from a large state in the country. Brijesh apparently came from a feudal background. As the story went, his well-educated father had intentionally denied him a decent education, fearing that worldly refinements would divorce Brijesh from the crudeness required to uphold the old order. Brijesh had fulfilled his father's ambitions admirably and was known for his strong-arm tactics. He had already made a mark for himself in public life at the state level and was now pursuing his ambitions in the capital city. He used to walk with a group of hangers-on, usually boisterous and loud. Over a period, Avinash and Brijesh came to acknowledge each other with a nod. The trees seemed wary of Brijesh, but it appeared to Avinash that they could not set the dogs on him because Brijesh always walked with a big group. Even the 'unseen people' seemed to hurriedly disappear with quick steps whenever they saw this group. Avinash learnt from his friends in the park that Mahapal's wife, Janaki Singh, was very unlike him. She was apparently well-educated, cultured and full of refinement. Moreover, she was a patron of the folk art of her region in a big way.

Then Janaki Singh suddenly died one day. She had apparently fallen down from the window of the tenth floor of the apartment block the couple lived in. There was a big hue and cry in the media and most people suspected foul play. Brijesh Mahapal was adamant it was an accidental fall. He swore that he had the best relations with his wife. But Janaki Singh's parents had serious doubts. They wanted a case of murder to be registered against Mahapal. They believed that nobody could accidentally fall off from a window just like that. The demand for a thorough investigation gained steam. The local police finally registered a murder case. Then, there was a clamour for a probe by an independent agency. The case was transferred to Avinash's investigation agency, and he was assigned the role of the supervisory officer.

By the time Avinash and his team took over the investigation, it was nearly a week after the incident. Avinash knew that it is the golden rule of investigation that the evidence you collect when you first visit the scene of crime is the best evidence. Evidence gets destroyed with every passing minute. In this case, Avinash's team first had to scrutinize the case records of the investigation conducted by the local police who were the initial responders, and thereafter revisit the scene of the offence and look for fresh clues. The facts gleaned from the police records were fairly simple. As per the post-mortem report, Janaki Singh had died of extensive head, thoracic, spinal and abdominal injuries. Most were skeletal injuries. To Avinash, it appeared consistent with death due to fall from a height. According to the statement of the husband given to the police, only he and his wife were present in the house on the day of the incident. His statement further mentioned that the apartment had large French windows, with only glass shutters. The windows had wide ledges capable of seating people. Janaki Singh was apparently in the habit of sitting on the ledge every day with the window open, taking in fresh air and listening to music. On that fateful day, after finishing her daily chores, she had gone through the same routine, sitting on the ledge of her bedroom window. Brijesh Mahapal had claimed in his statement that, in fact, he did not even know that his wife had fallen to her death, till he was informed by the apartment security staff, who had found Janaki Singh's body in a pool of blood on the ground. The statement of the security staff appeared to corroborate this fact. The couple had no children, although they had been married for over twelve years. The domestic help, Chandan Singh, was allegedly on leave on the day of the incident and had returned only the next day. Janaki Singh had not left behind any suicide note and her family members strongly believed that she was mentally very strong and would never have taken such a drastic step.

In a nutshell, there were no eyewitnesses to the incident, no evidence of any scuffle, and no ante-mortem injuries of the nature which raised the suspicion of a prior physical assault on Janaki Singh. The only other point of interest for Avinash was the crime scene photographs taken by the police. The photographs showed the pictures of the room from which the victim had allegedly fallen, her dead body where it lay on the ground and the profile of the apartment building to indicate the height from the tenth floor. Another notable feature in the crime scene photographs was the presence of a rather large dog of a mixed pedigree, mostly of Bhutia stock, greyish, with a bushy tail. It was present in many photographs and was especially prominent next to the dead body of Janaki Singh, sitting with its head resting on its paws. It appeared as if the dog was very attached to the victim and was distraught by her death.

Next, Avinash's team visited the scene of the incident as part of their own investigation. When they reached the apartment, they were surprised to find Brijesh Mahapal in the process of shifting his home! When asked the reason, Brijesh replied that he could not bear the sorrow of his wife's death and the fond memories of her which the house held. The site inspection finding by Avinash was largely consistent with the evidence that the police had collected. One more potential witness, the domestic help Chandan Singh was also present in the house. Avinash decided to record his statement later in the office. Brijesh Mahapal's version to Avinash's team was consistent with what he had told the police. But there was something about his demeanour; he looked timid and anxious, he was not the same boisterous Brijesh Mahapal of the park. Before leaving, Avinash asked him about the dog in the crime scene photos since he did not see it in the apartment. Brijesh appeared very startled by this question and replied rather defensively that he had already sent him to the new residence. He informed that Rocky, which was the dog's name, was greatly attached to his wife and was mourning her loss a great deal and hence he thought a change of place would do him good.

Avinash's team now proceeded to record the statements of the domestic help Chandan Singh, Mahapal's neighbours in the apartment complex and the parents of the victim. One lead which clearly emerged from all their statements was the fact that Brijesh Mahapal was a cruel husband and there was not much love lost between the husband and the wife. Domestic clashes were frequent, and mostly because Brijesh blamed his wife for not bearing any children.

Janaki Singh had related her plight on many occasions to her parents and neighbours. In short, given this evidence, Avinash felt that the theory of accidental fall needed much closer scrutiny. Avinash decided to conduct a dummy fall test with the help of a forensic team. The dummy fall test, Avinash knew, was not a fully scientific test and had no evidentiary value as such, but it was a tool of investigation. In this test, a dummy of the same size, weight and proportions as the victim is dropped from the same spot to see if the landing and the injuries are similar to that of the actual victim. His team simulated two falls; one with a hard push from the window and another with the mildest of touches. The position of Janaki Singh's body and the nature of her injuries appeared more consistent with the hard push in the dummy fall test. The experiment indicated that Janaki Singh could have been pushed from the window. While this experiment was in no way conclusive, it was an important turn of events in the case since prima facie, there were no clear reasons to suspect foul play by Brijesh Mahapal.

The next time Avinash interrogated Brijesh Mahapal, the latter had regained his confidence and was his boisterous old self. He vehemently denied any wrongdoing and alleged that the investigation was biased against him because of his reputation. Avinash informed him that if he thought so, he should cooperate with the agency in clearing his name by volunteering for a lie detector test. Brijesh replied that he would consult his lawyers and get back to the agency. A week or so later, Brijesh Mahapal sent a written reply to the investigation agency that he would not volunteer for the test, since his lawyers had advised that the test was unscientific and that the result of the test was not admissible evidence in a court of law.

At this point of time, the facts of the case before Avinash consisted of the statements of witnesses that there was marital discord between Brijesh and Janaki, the result of the dummy test showing some discrepancy in the theory of death by accidental fall, and the suspect's refusal to undergo a lie detector test. This was in no way sufficient to launch a successful prosecution against Brijesh Mahapal, although he was now clearly the prime suspect in the case.

Avinash decided that Brijesh Mahapal should be arrested and subjected to custodial interrogation. There was a possibility that he would disclose something useful during this process. So, an angry Brijesh Mahapal, in a threatening mood, was arrested and subjected to custodial interrogation by the agency. Nothing useful came out of this exercise since he was well-advised by his well-paid lawyers of on what to say to the agency. Soon, Brijesh got bail as the court felt that there was no compelling evidence to keep him in judicial custody. Avinash's team continued to struggle through the investigation, hoping for a miraculous breakthrough so that a successful prosecution could be launched against Brijesh.

Brijesh Mahapal was soon back in the park with his usual cronies. He now started hailing Avinash loudly in a sneering and mocking manner. Avinash was also surprised to see a massive dog which vaguely looked like Rocky walking furtively behind this motley group. The dog was never on a leash and the group appeared to be unaware of its presence, which Avinash thought was very negligent, since it was a burly dog and could attack strangers. But it appeared to him as if the dog was following the group in a rather strange manner, as if unable to make up its mind on something.

It was around two months after his release from the jail that Avinash got to know of Brijesh Mahapal's death in the famous park! There were some eye-witnesses who saw the entire incident happen in front of them. Brijesh was said to be walking alone that day. There is a narrow, elevated archway in the middle of the park which is at a fair height from the ground. Brijesh Mahapal was suddenly attacked by a big ferocious dog while walking on this archway, and in an effort to escape from it, he had fallen down and broken his neck. Death was instantaneous. There were many people in the park who had seen the entire sequence of events.

The last formality for Avinash's team now was collecting Brijesh Mahapal's death certificate and recording the statement of his dependents as proof of his death and submit the records to the court to close the case against him. Avinash went to Brijesh's new apartment for this purpose with his team and the domestic help Chandan Singh was also present there, along with others. Soon, Avinash's team completed the formalities and before leaving, Avinash asked Chandan Singh about Rocky, since he did not see him in the house.

After some hesitation, Chandan Singh replied, 'Sir, Rocky was killed by saheb the very next day after madam passed away! I don't know why, but he drugged him first and then battered him to death with an iron rod and threw his body in the pond in the big park the same night!' Avinash thought that Brijesh Mahapal had brutally killed the only eyewitness to the murder of his wife, although that eyewitness was not capable of any testimony in a human court of law. Avinash was very curious to speak to the eyewitnesses on Brijesh Mahapal's death in the park, to know more about the ferocious dog that had attacked him. They described the dog as a big greyish-coloured dog of Bhutia stock, with a bushy tail! When Avinash showed them the pictures of Rocky from the original crime scene photographs, they said it could be him!

Nobody has since seen the large greyish dog of Bhutia stock with a bushy tail in the famous park in the capital city of the country.

Little Khairi Still Roams the Wilds

The national park sprawled over an extensive area from the Gangetic plains to the lesser Himalayas, but was fragmented at many places due to the expansion of towns and the development of new roads. It was quite rich in bio-diversity, perhaps one of the few habitats where both the Himalayan Black Bear and the Sloth Bear co-existed during certain times of the year. Dhara forest outpost was located in the heart of the national park and was its most remote outpost. The outpost building was situated on high ground and commanded an all-round view of the forest below. The outpost complex comprised two tiny rooms and a toilet for the forest staff. It was basic accommodation with minimum amenities. The national park fell within Avinash's police range, but the police rarely ventured into the park. It was the exclusive domain of the forest department.

Avinash was fortunate that the park warden Kedar Mehta was a close friend. He sometimes joined Kedar on his patrolling rounds of the park. Their favourite destination was always the Dhara outpost. For Avinash, the night trips were the best. The duo used to get into Kedar's jeep after an early dinner, drive through the heart of the forest and reach Dhara. Once there, they would spend an hour or two listening to the sounds of the jungle. There were always elephants around Dhara, since there was a groundwater seepage just behind the outpost, which held water throughout the year. This had created a grassland habitat, which was irresistible to the elephants, especially in summer. Avinash and Kedar would invariably hear their squeals of delight during their nightly peregrinations to this spot. The most common sound of the jungle around Dhara, however, was the sawing call of the leopards. Dhara had high leopard density. On a few memorable occasions, they also heard the awe-inspiring 'Aaaaungh, Aaaaungh' of the roar of a tiger! A trip to Dhara always rejuvenated Avinash.

The outpost was manned by the forest staff throughout the year. They performed multifarious duties. Mainly, it was patrolling the forest on foot to prevent poaching or illegal tree felling, preventing the entry of stray cattle, maintaining water holes and controlling forest fires. It was a lonely life for the forest guards posted at Dhara. They were cut off from civilization for the most part of the year. Even fetching supplies from the nearby town for their own use was fraught with risks in the elephant-ridden forest. Their rickety motorcycles were charged at by the elephants quite often; a favourite pastime of the behemoths!

Umesh Nautiyal and Mohan Bhandari were the permanent forest guards stationed at Dhara. They were responsible for the protection of the forest and the wildlife under their jurisdiction. It was an onerous job, given the vast area, limited resources and the dangers involved. Only during the fire season, which was peak summers, did they get a few extra hands, who were part-time employees of the forest department. Given the gravity of the fire challenge in the dry jungle, even the few extra hands were highly inadequate.

But Umesh Nautiyal and Mohan Bhandari were always cheerful and self-motivated. They considered the national park their home. Most importantly, they enjoyed their jobs. Whenever Avinash and Kedar visited Dhara, they both were very happy to see them. Umesh and Mohan were always full of interesting stories of wildlife movements, narrow escapes from sloth bears and elephants during their patrols, and thrilling sightings of tigers. For Avinash, sitting under the moonlight, listening to their stories and hearing the forest sounds had a special quality to it. The dedication of the forest guards to their duty in such a remote outpost, far away from their own families, fraught with so many professional risks, was humbling. Umesh and Mohan were tough hill men and physically hard as nails. Years of spending their life in the forest had also given them a sixth sense about the presence of wildlife. They could even smell the presence of an elephant! Both Umesh and Mohan were pushing on in years, and by no means, young. But they always worked at improving their living conditions in that remote outpost. One interesting practice they adopted was growing vegetables in front of the outpost. Normally any cultivation in such a location would be fruitless, since it would be destroyed by the deer, wild pigs or elephants. But they carved a deep squarish hollow in the soil and planted vegetables there, just out of the reach of an elephant trunk! They used ladders to go down to work the patch and used the same technique to come up after harvesting their precious produce.

The national park was interspersed with many settlements of nomadic cattle herders. They had ceased being nomadic and become mostly settled jungle dwellers for generations now. They had huge herds of cattle which could graze in certain designated areas around the park. They sold milk and ghee in the nearby towns, transporting them on their motorcycles or bicycles. Due to their long stay in the forests, their jungle craft was well honed, and they were experts at evading troublesome elephants. But their activities caused major damage to the forests. Their cattle overgrazed, they lopped trees indiscriminately for fodder in a way that the trees did not regenerate properly again. And they polluted the forest water bodies with their daily activities. Due to all this, the relationship between the herders and the forest staff was always fraught and uneasy. However, in the interior outposts such as Dhara, the forest staff also depended on the pastoralists for their own supply of milk, ghee and other essentials. At the same time, they had a duty to ensure that the herders did not transgress the privileges available to them in the national park. The relationship between them was always a delicate balance.

It was on a March morning in 2008, just after the Holi festival, that Avinash received a message from the police control room that the pastoralists in the national park had gheraoed the Dhara forest outpost over the issue of a missing girl. The details were sketchy since there was no direct mobile or wireless link with Dhara. Not wanting to lose an opportunity to visit his favourite haunt, Avinash decided to proceed to the spot and attend to the problem. Once at Dhara, he was greeted by the sight of around a hundred men and women peacefully sitting in protest in front of the outpost. Umesh and Mohan were also present there, confabulating with the protesters.

Avinash's enquiries revealed that a young pastoralist girl named Khairi, along with her little brother had been grazing cattle in the periphery of the Dhara outpost the previous day. One of their milch buffaloes had strayed away from the herd and gone into the core area of the park. The girl had informed her brother that she would go to the outpost and seek help from the forest staff to round up the buffalo, before it is claimed by a passing tiger or some other carnivore. She had departed, leaving her brother behind and that was the last time anyone saw Khairi. She went missing thereafter. The little brother had gone home and informed his parents of the developments. But when the parents went to the outpost to enquire about Khairi, they were told that she had never visited the outpost. The herders were firmly convinced that there was some foul play behind Khairi's disappearance and the forest staff were involved. Avinash's interaction with old friends Umesh and Mohan revealed that they had gone to visit their families in the town for the Holi festival and had returned only that morning. In their absence, the outpost was manned by a temporary fire season hand, Khubchand. He completely denied that any girl from the settlement had visited the outpost the previous day. He suggested that Khairi must have become a victim of a tiger or a leopard attack.

Avinash soon gathered from the pastoralists that little Khairi, who was around fourteen years old, was born in the forests and had lived all her life with her parents and her younger brother in a hut in the nearby settlement just beyond the Dhara outpost. She was a happy, innocent child full of life and greatly attached to her family's herd of buffaloes. Being born in the forest, she was fearless and had roamed the wilds without a care in the world. Even the forest denizens seemed to have accepted her as a friend since she was never harmed. Every morning, she took the herds grazing to where the best pastures lay, gaily singing old pastoralist songs taught to her by her grandmother.

Quite often, the buffaloes ventured near elephant herds during their grazing and Khairi was apparently totally nonchalant during such encounters and would giggle helplessly at the antics of the young elephant calves! Occasionally, she visited the nearby town riding on the back of her father's motorcycle. She was fascinated by the wares in the local bazar. Her two favourite destinations were the colourful clothes corner and the trinkets shop. But her father's meagre income was not sufficient to permit any reckless shopping forays on her part! Little Khairi never demanded anything, but her adoring father would sometimes indulge her fancy and buy her clothes of her choice, as also cheap imitation jewellery.

Avinash assured the herders that the police would conduct a thorough probe and make all efforts to recover Khairi. It was probable that the young girl had lost her way in the jungle. Moreover, there was no record of any man-eating tiger or leopard in the national park for a very long time. Avinash formed a mixed party of the forest staff, the police and the herders to search for Khairi and they all set out looking for her. One of the search parties was sometime later alerted by a congregation of vultures and crows on a tree and decided to investigate the reason. There, they stumbled upon the distressing remains of little Khairi in the thick undergrowth around two kilometres away from Dhara outpost. There was not much left of the poor unfortunate girl, since the scavengers of the forest had set to work in real earnest. Only the little girl's head was intact and Khairi, the innocent child of the wild had been reduced to a few pitiful bones. The police collected what remained of the girl for post-mortem examination to determine the cause of death. But Avinash knew from his experience that with such scanty remains, the doctors would not be able to give any conclusive opinion on the cause of her death. From the inspection of the spot, his suspicion was aroused since he did not find Khairi's clothes or other personal effects like jewellery, etc., near the body. Thorough search of the surrounding areas also did not yield any results. Thereafter the police party came back to the Dhara outpost and Avinash decided to conduct a minute search of the premises for potential clues. But to him, it appeared as if the entire premises had been recently swept clean and washed thoroughly in a very deliberate manner. However, during the search, in the corner of the room where Khubchand lived, a tiny fragment of glass of indeterminate colour caught his eye. It looked like the shard of a broken glass bangle. Umesh and Mohan were very certain that no woman had visited the outpost as long as they could remember. Khairi's distraught mother disclosed that the little girl was very fond of bangles and always wore red coloured ones.

Avinash felt that the police now needed to thoroughly interrogate Khubchand. He was the only person present at the outpost on the previous day, since the alibi of Umesh and Mohan of having visited their families for Holi was confirmed upon verification. Khubchand was very vehement in denying any association with the fate of the unfortunate girl and strongly reiterated that Khairi had never visited the outpost. But Avinash found his behaviour rather evasive and suspicious. Avinash felt that if only the police could have recovered Khairi's bangles from the spot where her body was found, a forensic test could have been conducted to match the shard recovered in Khubchand's room. It appeared to him that somebody had clearly tampered with the evidence in a methodical manner. Both Umesh and Mohan knew very little about Khubchand and his past or even his background.

Avinash then decided that the police would register a case of murder against unknown persons and conduct a proper investigation into the death of Khairi. Before leaving Dhara, he took Umesh and Mohan into confidence and told them to try to get Khubchand to talk in the evening and see if he discloses anything of interest about the incident. He also deputed a police team to further interrogate Khubchand and keep a watch over him, and also search the surrounding forest areas in the daylight thoroughly for Khairi's clothes and other belongings.

However, the very next morning, Avinash received the shocking information that Khubchand had purportedly been mauled and killed by a tiger! He left immediately for Dhara. Upon arrival, he found Khubchand's blood-soaked body not far from the Dhara outpost itself. Umesh narrated the circumstances of the entire incident to Avinash. After Avinash had left the previous evening from Dhara, towards dusk, a buffalo was heard bellowing in the jungle close to the outpost and Umesh had told Khubchand to round it up and bring it to the outpost. Khubchand had gone looking for the buffalo, but did not return for a long time. He did not even answer their calls. The police party stationed at Dhara failed to locate him after searching the area thoroughly. In the morning, Umesh and Mohan had again launched a search and had discovered Khubchand's dead body in the dense undergrowth quite close to the outpost. Avinash soon examined the dead body, which had almost been ripped apart, but also bore two clean puncture wounds on the throat, a seemingly classic tiger kill! This was perhaps the first instance of a tiger killing a human being in the history of the national park! The body was otherwise untouched, and the tiger had made no attempt to consume the flesh. But what caught Avinash's attention were the objects lying around Khubchand's dead body. Those were girl's clothes tied up in a bundle and red bangle fragments strewn all around! It was quite clear that somebody had deliberately collected and thrown these objects in that spot. Of the buffalo which had bellowed, there were no further signs! Now, there was nothing further that the police could do about Khubchand, who had died a ghastly death.

Even though it was now only of academic interest, Avinash decided to get the bangle fragments recovered from that spot matched in the forensic laboratory with the glass shard recovered from Khubchand's room the previous day. The forensic report came after two weeks, which stated that the material and the composition of the glass shard had matched with the bangles and that there was a high probability that they were manufactured in the same batch! As Avinash had expected, the post-mortem examination report of Khairi's mortal remains were inconclusive on the cause of death. If Khubchand had lived and had been prosecuted for murder, there was a possibility of his acquittal since the cause of Khairi's death was not clear and the forensic evidence would only have been circumstantial in nature.

But justice, in a sense, had already been done for little Khairi. Avinash believed that she must have taken the matter into her own hands since the young girl probably had no faith in the police and their archaic ways of ensuring justice.

Strangely, there have been no more human kills by tigers in the national park since then. Umesh Nautiyal and Mohan Bhandari have both retired now and occasionally call Avinash to enquire about his well-being. He has also learnt from them, that of late, the area of Dhara outpost has seen an explosion in tiger numbers. Avinash feels that they are all under little Khairi's care now!

The Old Office after Midnight

The two massive cream and red sandstone office blocks were the ultimate seat of power in the capital city of the country. Avinash always felt as if the personalities of the imposing sandstone edifices constantly altered! At times they looked lifeless, just a huge complex of impressive stone structures, and at other times, it seemed as if they came alive, like a living, breathing entity! He felt that the time of the day also seemed to make a difference to the way the structures looked. In the day time, they were striking and well-disposed of, but at night, they still looked striking, but distant and sombre! The mood of the weather also appeared to reflect on the mood of the two blocks – warm, cold and sometimes brooding!

There was a time, slightly over a decade ago, when Avinash worked in a ministry in one of the blocks of this sandstone complex. On his first day in the office, the structure had felt very impersonal and intimidating. As if he were an interloper! Was it really the building? Or was it the people in the building? Avinash wasn't sure.

Avinash, being a mere police officer, had no business working in the ministry in such a grand old office! Such jobs were usually the preserve of more qualified people. But occasionally, certain complex jobs demanded specific domain expertise and Avinash accidentally ended up with such a job in the ministry. However, he found it very easy to grasp the intricacies of his new assignment. Years of experience in policing gave him insights into his new work, which others perhaps did not enjoy. Since he was also aware of the practical ground realities, having worked in the field, his policy formulations had a good impact. Avinash was soon accepted as a freak success; an exception to the general rule, by the more highly qualified people! In reality, he immensely enjoyed the work in the ministry due to its diversity of exposure and the immediate impact of his interventions on the ground. Also, he found the massive sandstone office blocks immensely interesting for many other reasons!

Having settled down into his new job, he soon started exploring the precincts of the sandstone blocks and found many intriguing characteristics in the seemingly lifeless collection of stones. There were subterranean chambers, mysterious alleyways, abandoned domes and peculiar corridors! Also, strange odours, unexplained gusts of wind and shadowy movements! Office papers were lost in these buildings in the most curious manner, from time to time. Strange people, claiming to be office staff and media personnel, lurked behind the pillars in the silent corridors. And, very soon, in these ethereal settings, Avinash felt at home. The ethereal quality of his new office was also accentuated by three other celestial features of the sandstone blocks – the office boys, the files and the meetings!

The enduring category of people permanently inhabiting this entire complex were the office boys or the peons. They sat in front of every office room in ancient chairs. If one looked at them closely, one realized that they were not boys anymore, but were quite grown up. Almost all of them had more or less similar demeanours and expressions on their faces. They knew about everything that happened inside those closed office rooms. They were prescient, to the extent of almost being clairvoyant, since they were familiar with all the files and what was inside them! They could even predict the outcome of each file. They had seen it all. They were the eyes and ears of the sandstone complex. They had been in these buildings nearly all their lives, while others had come and gone. They knew the alleyways and the strange short-cuts from one block of the building to another. Sometimes they talked in conspiratorial whispers about the purported next shift of office boys, who took over as darkness fell. The office boys had close bonds with the files they carried every day, every hour from one desk to the other. They could even recognize the files as if they were people!

Then there were the files! In reality, the entire complex was 'the kingdom of files'. The files came with their own unique personalities. Some were old and orphaned; they had been around a long time with no outcomes. A large number of files meandered along, up and down, at times aimlessly as if they belonged to the in-between-world. Neither here nor there. Then there were the hot files. They galloped at express speed. They were the glamour boys of the kingdom of files. There were also some files, which defied logic; they originated normally, continued to exist normally and then charged at breakneck speed, when the boss screamed. The office boys empathized equally with all the files. But their favourites were the files belonging to the in-between-world! They were proud of them, since the files of the in-between-world conformed to precise rules and office orders; the hallmark of a perfect system, of which the office boys had been a part all their lives, sometimes even for generations.

Then there were the meetings! The meetings in the sandstone complex were all 'Extremely Important Meetings'. An officer holding many such meetings, especially at odd hours, immediately went up in the estimation of the office boys. At any given time, there were many Extremely Important Meetings happening. Everybody felt very proud to be part of such meetings. The cogitations were intense. The views expressed were unequivocal. It was a constant education to be part of such Extremely Important Meetings. The deliberations were often in abstract terms, not overly burdened by practical considerations of reality, as all Extremely Important Meetings should be. The outcomes were never hasty. Years of institutional wisdom mandated more deliberations for utmost clarity of purpose and action. It was the quality of the journey and not the destination which was important. Avinash came out of such meetings greatly enriched by the experience. There was almost a nostalgic urge in him to attend more such meetings in the future, preferably on the same subject!

Once he embraced the aura of the sandstone building and grasped the intricate celestial interplay of the files, the meetings and the office boys, Avinash felt invincible. He actually felt as if he was supernaturally endowed! He soon started pouring scorn on people who came for meetings from lesser buildings. It was a constant high for him from morning to night.

Avinash was always curious to know what happened in the sandstone blocks in the night when the doors were shut. The office boys had mysteriously hinted about the second shift. Who came for the second shift? The office boys were evasive. But thankfully, he did not have to wait for too long to find out. The opportunity came knocking, as if the seemingly lifeless sandstones had read his mind!

Avinash still remembers that day clearly; it had started in a routine manner. He had presided over an Extremely Important Meeting on the subject of 'Important matters pending for more than ten years'. It was a good meeting, and the participants had bounced a lot of ideas and he had felt very happy with the outcome. Avinash had decided that the matter needed more deliberations for further clarity. Soon, he received an order that he had to do the control room shift duty from 1200 hours midnight to 0800 hours the next morning. There had been a serious law and order incident in a particular state and all the officers were required to be present in the control room in shifts to monitor the situation and report any fresh developments to the higher authorities. Avinash was assigned the midnight shift and his ardent desire to visit the building at night was fulfilled! He left the office, had an early dinner and decided to take a short nap, and set the alarm clock for 11.45 p.m.

When Avinash reached the office block at midnight, it looked very different. The immediate feature he noticed was the complete absence of cars and people. Also, the shadows from myriad lights created strange elongated shapes. There was a furtive movement of hazy figures in the domes, perhaps of security guards. The silence in the entire complex was deafening. As he walked in to enter the building, all the lights on the first floor suddenly came to life! At the entrance, the security guard was slouched in his chair with his gun next to him, as if in a deep slumber. Avinash's efforts to wake him up were met with a momentary opening of the eyes and a nod and the guard closed his eyes again, oblivious to the world.

The control room was on the ground floor and Avinash tiptoed there cautiously through the lonely corridor. All the TV sets in the control room panel were switched on and were showing the news in the mute mode. There was no one present there and Avinash fervently hoped that the duty officer had gone to relieve himself. He watched the TV panels, all showing the same news of the law and order incident, which had warranted his shift duty. Soon, he heard the faint chatter of people talking on the first floor where the main conference room was situated. His curiosity got the better of him and he climbed the staircase and reached the first floor to see what was happening. Strangely, there were a few office boys sitting in the chairs in front of the closed office rooms. Avinash could not recognize any of them and they did not bother to acknowledge him either. Surprisingly, there was a meeting in progress in the main conference room! But Avinash could not identify any of the participants as he entered inside to check what was happening. The participants wore attires that had gone long out of fashion, perhaps half a century ago, and their accents and verbal expressions were suggestive of an era long gone by! It was as if Avinash had travelled back in time. He quietly sat on a chair to observe their deliberations and in the beginning, the participants of the meeting completely ignored him. Soon Avinash became extremely uneasy with this entire experience and wanted to converse with the participants to get a grip of the situation. He introduced himself to them and all of a sudden, they seemed to notice him. In a slow and deliberate manner, all the participants started to converge towards Avinash, and he, now thoroughly rattled, rushed out of the conference room. As he ran out, he could just barely discern the agenda item written on an ancient blackboard 'Important matters pending for more than ten years'!

Suddenly the alarm went off and Avinash woke up with a start from his nap! It was time for his shift duty! As he entered the office building, the security guard was slouched in his chair, fast asleep and the lights suddenly came to life on the first floor! Walking gingerly, he proceeded towards the control room. All the TV screens are switched on and were showing the news in the mute mode! The duty officer was missing. Then he heard indistinct chatter from the first floor. Avinash climbed the stairs nervously and found the entire corridor empty, except for the main conference room. A seemingly tall, gaunt and skeletal-looking office boy with sunken eyes was sitting in the chair outside and a meeting appeared to be in progress! Curious, Avinash wanted to see the proceedings inside, but the office boy firmly refused to let him inside, insisting that he was not an invitee to the meeting!

Finding the entire experience eerie and uncanny, Avinash came down the stairs and proceeded to the control room. Thankfully, the duty officer was back. After recovering from his strange experience, Avinash casually asked the duty officer to check if anyone was holding a meeting upstairs. The duty officer looked a little surprised and went up and came back a little while later and informed Avinash that all the lights were switched on in the main conference room, but there was no one, just empty coffee cups on the table! The duty officer believed that apparently, there must have been a meeting recently, but the participants had probably just left in a hurry!

Avinash did not offer any views and completed his shift duty and returned home. Also, he decides that in the future, he would not display any more ardour for night shift duties in the old sandstone office blocks!

Do Miracles Really Happen Anymore?

After an evening meal, you recline in a comfortable chair on the terrace of the house and gaze pensively outside. The sky is brilliant with a million stars twinkling brightly. Just outside the house, maybe two hundred meters away, runs a small river and in the still of the night, you can hear its soft gurgle as it ripples and bubbles over the rocks. All that separates the house from the river is a raised embankment, on top of which is a low iron fence. Beyond the river is a steep ridge with thick undergrowth interspersed with trees. As you close your eyes and enjoy the crisp mountain breeze, suddenly from somewhere across the ridge, a barking deer sets off its strident alarm call; a predator is on the move!

Soon it is time for you to go to sleep and the barking deer alarm call slowly fades farther and farther away into a distance as you shut your eyes. Then, suddenly, sometime in the middle of your slumber, you are woken up by the distinct sawing call of a leopard! Now, the barking deer gets hysterical again with fear and calls out for all the world to hear, and the still night resonates with its harsh call. Slowly, the din dies down, and you shut your eyes again and wake up refreshed the next morning, to the soothing call of the red jungle fowl, announcing a beautiful new day!

Avinash was fortunate enough to have lived in such a lovely place; a valley town in the Sivaliks in a hill state, where he was posted as a senior police officer some years ago. The house in which Avinash lived was located in the police complex, next to the small river, Munipana.

Avinash had mixed feelings about his new assignment as the chief of police in the hill state. He was always the happiest while tackling difficult policing challenges which called for ingenuity. The present assignment was essentially in a very peaceful place, but with a history of minor matters being blown out of proportion! The policing challenges, therefore, were largely predictable and consisted of mostly dousing non-existent fires! But to make up for the absence of serious policing challenges, Avinash was often required to put down unseemly squabbles among his own officers, which was a peculiar feature of this assignment! Once Avinash set his own house in order, the professional work was largely routine and not unduly challenging. But the Himalayan state had much to offer by way of compensation for lack of serious work, with its majestic natural beauty and bio-diversity. The range of landscapes extended from the permanent snowline to the unforgettable terai forests, where the tiger still reigned supreme. So, his normally restless persona was somewhat anchored by the bounty of nature all around. And the police colony where Avinash lived with other officers and men was like no other place, in terms of its beautiful natural setting and the quality of infrastructure. It was simply a joy to live there.

The location of the police complex also had a rather curious past. It was considered the worst possible parcel of land and was allocated to the police department to build dwelling units for its personnel. It was a rocky wasteland, in fact an old river bed; Munipana having changed her course over the years. At some point of time, the land had served as an ancient burial ground, with all the attendant superstitions which go with such a setting. But the police had to make do with whatever they got!

However, in just a few years, by sheer dint of grit, determination and imagination, the police department had transformed the rocky wasteland into a comfortable haven. The dwelling units were broadly of two kinds – big houses for the officers in one cluster and smaller houses for the other ranks in another cluster. The difference in the standards between the two categories of houses was rather stark, and Avinash often felt that the families and children of his subordinate colleagues resented this distinction. But the redeeming feature of the colony was the common playground, where all the children played together, regardless of the ranks of their parents.

The river Munipana, which flowed in front of the colony, originated in the Sivaliks and was seasonal. But in the monsoons, Munipana was a sight to behold, cascading with a fury seen to be believed, with the lower part of the colony being under considerable threat of being washed away every year. But fortunately, it never happened. Even in the dry months, whenever there was a heavy downpour, Munipana was prone to flash floods with rocks clattering down, as myriad mountain streams drained into it. It was not uncommon to see wild boar or barking deer perish in the wake of such flash floods and being washed ashore. The ridge beyond Munipana was given protection by the police department and extensively planted with local flora every monsoon. Soon, wildlife made a remarkable comeback with even leopards being fairly common. There was a walking path in the colony adjacent to Munipana, all along its embankment for around half a kilometre. In the early mornings and late evenings, one could sight barking deer, wild boar or an occasional leopard just across the river, only a few metres away as one walked!

Avinash had got a waterhole made on the banks of Munipana and in the summer months, it became the favourite destination for all the wildlife around. An exceptionally bold leopard was a frequent visitor and one could see him sitting fearlessly and staring at people as they walked. But the leopard never crossed the low embankment and entered the colony during the daytime.

Occasionally, after the monsoon rains or a flash flood, an old skeleton would lie slightly exposed on the banks of Munipana – the relics of the old burial ground! They would be given a quick burial at the spot by the police. The children of the colony, who always played in the river would heap rocks over them, which soon became large piles of stones. The children sometimes placed flowers on such heaps, all in the course of their play.

The children were the heart and soul of the police complex. All ranks blurred when they played together, which they did from the morning to the night! The ringing laughter of children resonated throughout the colony giving it a special energy. The river was one of their favourite haunts; to splash around when there was water or to build all kinds of castles with sand or stone, when the river was dry.

At times, it was incongruous to hear children shouting and laughing, with the sound of barking deer alarm calls in the background! But the children always came home safe and sound. Anxious parents scolded them constantly not to play in the river, what with a leopard lurking in the corner and the fear of a flash flood, but the children didn't seem to care as they were always there near Munipana, with some new game or the other.

But constable Manoj Rawat never scolded his only son Prashant. He was always extremely gentle with him. Prashant was around twelve years old and autistic. It was not apparent when you saw Prashant, with his aquiline hill features and striking good looks. But little Prashant had serious difficulties with social interactions and communication. He was prone to repetitive behaviour patterns and he would never make eye contact with anyone. Manoj Rawat and his wife took good care of Prashant, who was under treatment with specialists. However, Prashant never mixed with other children and would play all alone along the river after everyone had left. His favourite game was heaping more stones on the old graves, which he did with almost an obsessive regularity. He seemed happy and content in his little world, which he seemed to guard zealously. Avinash used to see him playing in the river, with Manoj or his wife keeping a close eye on him. Prashant seemed to have exceptional sensory perceptions and some kind of communion with nature. Avinash would often see him going very near barking deer fawns, who did not seem to fear him at all. On one particular day, Avinash saw Prashant looking intensely at what turned out to be the exceptionally bold leopard in the water hole, with Manoj Rawat frantically running to get him back! For just a fleeting moment,

Prashant made eye contact with Avinash and smiled, and continued looking at the leopard.

Manoj Rawat was a traffic constable. His salary was a meagre forty thousand rupees or so per month. He also had to take care of his parents and younger siblings in a remote mountain village with this income. Prashant's treatment was a financial strain on him, but he and his wife were completely devoted to Prashant and spared no expenditure on his treatment. The work of a traffic constable is tough. Standing for upto ten to twelve hours a day throughout the week takes a toll on the knees and the ankle with many orthopaedic ailments developing over time. In addition, breathing foul air constantly due to emissions from vehicles affected the lungs. To make matters worse, the public often misbehaved with traffic police personnel during enforcement of traffic rules. So, all in all, it was a stressful job, both physically and mentally. Manoj Rawat was an ideal traffic constable; he was fit, well turned-out, polite in his dealings with the public and very firm when he was required to enforce the rules. Sometimes Avinash used to marvel how policemen like Manoj Rawat maintained such high levels of motivation and probity with such meagre salary and limited avenues for promotion. A small reward or a generous praise was all they needed to keep going.

One day, there was a flash flood in Munipana and this time, the skeleton of a small child lay partially exposed on the river bed. All the children saw it, but Prashant soon reached there and shooed them off. Avinash saw him digging a hole in the sand to bury the small, forlorn skeleton. Soon he started heaping stones over it till Manoj, who was watching the proceedings, called him back as it was getting dark. From that day onwards, the grave of the small child was Prashant's special destination; the stone heap soon acquiring formidable proportions. He placed flowers over it every day. At times, Avinash would see him standing there, talking in low tones, as if to a friend! Whenever Avinash walked along the child's grave, he felt as if he could smell the fragrance of incense sticks wafting in the air, although he could never find its source. Maybe it was just his imagination, but sometimes he thought that he could hear the sweet and distant sound of a child singing softly as he crossed the grave! Due to Prashant's constant efforts, the pile of stones on the grave had grown to nearly four feet in height.

Then one terrible October evening, without a warning, it happened. There must have been a cloudburst in the upper reaches of the hills, and in the blink of an eye, the gentle Munipana was transformed into a raging torrent. Before Manoj Rawat could react, Prashant, who was playing near the little child's grave was caught in the flash flood. The doctors had told Manoj Rawat that autistic children find it difficult to cope with unfamiliar external stimuli and are prone to react with extreme agitation when it happens. In the face of the wrathful Munipana, Prashant had little chance as Manoj watched the events unfold before his own eyes from the embankment, horrified and helpless. His cries soon brought other inhabitants of the colony to the scene, but no one could help, since the speed and volume of water in the river was fearsome. In the meantime, somebody called the disaster rescue force. Prashant somehow barely managed to get on top of the little child's grave and hung on tenaciously to a big rock. But the deluge of the raging Munipana soon drowned the grave, with the debris battering everything in its wake. Nothing could have survived such an onslaught by the elements. Before the disaster rescue force could arrive twenty-five minutes later, it was all over. As the water began to recede, Prashant walked out of the river miraculously, calm and unscathed through all the flood and fury!

There was no logical explanation how Prashant had survived the onslaught of the irate Munipana. But he did so, without a single scratch. There was also no explanation as to how he could remain so calm and composed under such an intense flood-burst, given his condition.

The next day, as Avinash walked along the Munipana, he saw the little child's grave adorned with beautiful fresh flowers. And there was the sweet and mysterious smell of incense wafting in the air!

The Village Priest of Bettagrama

Avinash had known Parameshwara Bhatt all his life. In fact, the latter had always been a part of Avinash's family in a peripheral sense, since Parameshwara Bhatt was the priest of the village temple of Bettagrama, where his family had lived for generations. There was little change in Parameshwara Bhatt's appearance from the time Avinash first saw him as a child, to the present, although more than fifty years had elapsed in between! He was the longest-serving priest of Bettagrama village and was highly regarded by the villagers for his integrity and rectitude. Parameshwara Bhatt was also a classic introvert and spoke very little. But he always conveyed a sense of warmth to anyone who interacted with him through his eyes, without saying too much.

Avinash's village, Bettagrama, nestled in the Central Western Ghats in the state of Karnataka. The defining physical feature of his village was a large hillock called the Balya Betta, which towered over the village. Balya Betta, in local parlance, meant the "big hillock" and

Bettagrama meant the "village with a hillock". It was rumoured that Avinash's forefathers had settled in Bettagrama village more than three hundred years ago, due to its wonderful quality of mountain air, which was said to be unparalleled. Bettagrama was a large village in terms of size; the northern border marked by the Balya Betta and the southern border by a small perennial river, Kadpole, which meant the 'wild' or the 'untamed river' in local language. The distance between Kadpole to the foothills of Balya Betta was around two kilometres and it was often possible to walk from one end of the village to the other, without meeting anyone! The homesteads in Bettagrama were widely dispersed; each family with its own neat red-tiled house, a small coffee grove, and patches of rice fields. The houses generally overlooked the coffee groves and the rice fields. The social interaction between the villagers of Bettagrama was limited and happened mostly during the village festivals or on occasions like weddings or funerals. Bettagrama was a good village with good people and disputes of any nature were almost unknown. Avinash's house was situated at the far southern corner of the village, close to the river Kadpole. The village was intersected in the middle by a well-maintained strip of public road, which ran from Kadpole river to the foothills of Balya Betta.

A walk along this road from the banks of Kadpole river to Balya Betta and thereafter climbing the steep hillock was a favourite pastime of Avinash when he was young. He could cover the entire distance in less than forty minutes! He would start the journey from his house, turn left, reach the Kadpole river a short distance away, then turn back and walk along the same road again. The Kadpole river, which coursed through ancient volcanic rock beds, had crystal clear water throughout the year, except during the monsoons, when she became a raging torrent with fearsome flotsams and jetsams!

On the banks of river Kadpole was a small red-tiled house belonging to Chandra. He had the quaint job of measuring the water levels of Kadpole periodically and sending the reports to the central government! He was part of the national flood control set up and received a small honorarium for his troubles. After starting from the river, Avinash would walk along the village road, on both sides of which were mostly coffee groves with ancient evergreen shade trees. Invariably, in the mornings and the evenings, all along the route, Avinash would be greeted by mellifluous bird song or at other times, by the orchestrated chirping of cicadas, especially during the monsoons. His house was a short distance from Kadpole, along the road. It was an old rambling house, over a hundred years old, built by Avinash's great-grandfather. Somehow, successive generations of the family had held it together and prevented it from crumbling! The house always conveyed a warm sense of belonging and security to Avinash. Over the years, the old house had sheltered and fostered generations of happy children. The house had also witnessed many deaths during its existence. Once past the old house, the next landmark along the route for Avinash was Bettagrama's sacred grove. It was a small patch of forest with grand trees, which were centuries old. No one was allowed to cut trees in the village sacred grove and it also housed a small forest shrine dedicated to a demi-god, Bote Aiyappa, where the villagers occasionally made offerings. After the sacred grove, Avinash's next destination was always his family's ancestral dwelling place; a further walk of around ten minutes from the sacred grove. It was a large house built more than two hundred years ago, with ornate doors and windows and an open courtyard inside. An old hanging brass lamp burned eternally in the main hall of the house. But alas, no family members lived there anymore, all having settled down over the years in their own individual homesteads. But once or twice a year, many family members congregated at the ancestral house to celebrate festivals and pay respects to departed elders. A compulsory destination for all the family members was the small family shrine situated next to the ancestral house, dedicated to a revered family elder.

Avinash had always found the scene from the portico of the family shrine very enchanting, as it unfolded before him. In front of the shrine, stretched endless rice fields swaying in the gentle breeze, interspersed with small ponds which shimmered in the sun light. The rice fields were bordered by patches of green groves all around. And in the far distance were the blue mountains of the Western Ghats. Just behind the shrine was the looming Balya Betta, almost at touching distance! Avinash always enjoyed the scent of forest flowers which invariably blew in the wind over the ancestor's shrine. After paying his obeisance to the family elder, his next destination was always the temple dedicated to the village deity. This temple was of hoary vintage, built of granite stones.

As Avinash entered the temple, he would invariably see Parameshwara Bhatt standing at the entrance, gazing into the horizon. Very few devotees visited the temple on a daily basis in Bettagrama. It came alive mostly during the village festivals. Parameshwara Bhatt would give Avinash a flicker of recognition and a warm smile, and mumble a greeting, for he was always a man of few words. He would do the aarti for Avinash, come out of the garbhagriha and stand again at the entrance and gaze at Avinash with his kindly eyes as he left.

Avinash would thank him and walk further and reach the foothills of Balya Betta. There was a narrow but steep footpath through thick undergrowth which took Avinash to the summit of Balya Betta, a climb of around 25 minutes. On the summit of Balya Betta was a tiny little temple dedicated to the deity of the hill. No one in Bettagrama clearly knew when it was built, but it was very old. The deity was the guardian angel of the village. The view from the top of the hill was breath-taking; distant cloud-kissed mountains in the horizon and verdant green groves with tiny villages in the valley in between. Avinash always spent some time at the summit, soaking in the mountain air, before slowly heading back home, pleasantly tired.

The entire journey from Kadpole to the top of Balya Betta would have taken him around forty minutes, but the quality of that journey would have added another forty minutes to his life, every time he walked!

Avinash's first memory of Parameshwara Bhatt was of perhaps when he was four or five years old. His grandfather used to organize pujas in the village temple during the summer holidays. The entire extended family, including the aunts, uncles and the cousins used to congregate in the village. Those were the best of times for Avinash and his siblings as they basked in the warm glow of their grandparents' affection, along with other family members. Parameshwara Bhatt invariably conducted those pujas for the family. For the children, the best part of the puja was the tasty prasad which he used to hand out and Avinash always got an extra portion! Parameshwara Bhatt lived near the village temple with his family and it was a pious and hardworking family. The income from his priestly duties was meagre, but he educated his children well and they subsequently got decent jobs, which eased his financial situation.

Avinash left Bettagrama for studies, when he was still young. Thereafter, he got into a career as a police officer, which kept him away from his village for long periods of time. But certain memories of his childhood in Bettagrama were deeply imprinted in his psyche and were simply unforgettable. He especially remembered the annual coffee flowering, the monsoon rains and the harvest festival with great fondness.

The coffee flowering! Avinash always loved how it happened suddenly, in the month of March every year! Without a warning, the thunderstorms broke, soaking the dry land, producing the scent of the gods, the petrichor, the sweet smell of rain falling on mother earth. The March thunderstorms were called the blossom showers; for eight days later, a miracle unfolded and the coffee bushes bloomed in a sea of white, with the fragrance of all that was good and pure. As Avinash stood under the ancient shade trees in the coffee grove and watched this marvel unfold every year, the birds sang, the bees made honey, the dry leaves rustled in the gentle breeze, and the sweet smell of coffee flowers lingered through the day and the night.

The monsoons usually set in Bettagrama by the end of May; and it wasn't long before dark ominous clouds built up, with bolts of lightning in a vivid searing flash, the claps of thunder, the trembling of the earth, and the howling of the winds! The ancient coffee shade trees braced themselves for the onslaught and rain poured in sheets of white. The rivers raged, the streams overflew, the paddy fields became a sea of water and Avinash's old house creaked and leaked! As the brooding majesty of monsoon unleashed itself, the earth healed, the rivers and streams replenished and the land wore a cloak of green, shiny and new. Nature at its most elemental, man at his most practical, working the land in the rice fields, a union as old as civilization! Avinash sometimes used to stand on the bridge over the Kadpole river under a battered umbrella, looking at the heavens – dark and foreboding; looking at the river – foaming and frothing; looking at the earth – green and freshly cleansed.

But Avinash's finest memory was of the harvest festival! On a glorious full moon night every year, towards the end of November or early December, a procession would wind its way from the old house, through the night-scented coffee groves to the paddy fields, illuminated by the silver moon. It was a procession of family members, farm helps, relatives and friends, all dressed in traditional finery. The lady of the house was always in the lead, a small flickering lamp cupped in her palms, and the path was always lit by burning bamboo torches. Soon, the procession would reach the paddy fields, the new season's paddy sheaves were cut and handed over to everyone, and an ancient chant rent the still night air; "O God, give us a bountiful harvest!" In the far corners of the horizon, such scenes were being enacted by other villagers – the burning bamboo torches and the immemorial chants – "O God, give us a bountiful harvest!" As the procession came back to the old house, the festivities started, and the fireworks began. Family and friends gathered around to the tinkle of warm laughter which carried far into the dew-drenched full moon night.

After Avinash entered into his professional career as a police officer, whenever he went back to Bettagrama on short visits, it was a regular ritual for him to visit the family shrine and the village temple. Parameshwara Bhatt would always be present in the village temple and it was as if he was almost an extension of the sacred temple. He would smile, mumble enquiries about Avinash's present whereabouts, and conduct the aarti. Then he would come out, stand at the entrance of the temple and look at Avinash in his quiet manner as the latter bid goodbye, till they met again.

Avinash always sensed a look of certain pride in Parameshwara Bhatt's eyes when he saw him, maybe because he had done fairly well in life. To Parameshwara Bhatt, Avinash was after all, a village lad of Bettagrama, who had done the village proud. Parameshwara Bhatt was growing in years and was nearing ninety, the last time Avinash had met him. Some of his grandchildren were already married.

This time around, Avinash could visit Bettagrama only after a long gap of over three years. But thankfully, as always, nothing had changed. On the very next day of his arrival, Avinash paid his customary visit to the family shrine and the village temple. The reassuring figure of Parameshwara Bhatt was standing at the entrance of the village temple, but he looked really old. This time, he merely smiled at Avinash and did not mumble his usual enquiries. Avinash finished the aarti and took leave of him, but Parameshwara Bhatt's gaze appeared very distant and far away. Avinash thought that perhaps old age was finally catching up with the temple priest.

When Avinash reached home, his father remarked that the new priest of the village temple was very young and had been recruited with great difficulty. "Nobody is willing to do priestly duties anymore," he remarked. Avinash asked his father, "What new priest?" Avinash's father replied, "Oh, I think I forgot to tell you, Parameshwara Bhatt passed away a couple of years ago; he was a good man and a fine priest"!

The Curious Case of the Class of 1986

It was in the winter of 2016 that Avinash attended the wedding reception of a colleague's son in the paramilitary facility located in the complex which was once the 'old campus' of a well-known university in the capital city – the university known for its intense debates and leftist ideology! In the days gone by, the university was located at two facilities, known as the 'old campus' and the 'new campus'. However, some years ago, the entire university had shifted to the present campus, hugging the outcrops of the Aravallis. The 'old' campus was converted into a government facility and allocated to various departments, including a paramilitary force, which subsequently became a much sought-after venue for wedding receptions and private parties. Wedding receptions tend to be tedious events, if one is not familiar with the guests. Beyond a point, the exchange of pleasantries and the customary smiles become a little forced. Fortunately, in the present instance, there was a bar and Avinash found succour in a couple of large drinks, which he gulped down in record time. He was waiting for a decent interval to make his departure not look too unseemly. It was only then that the realisation dawned on him, that the building where his post-graduation classes were held in the university was adjacent to the reception venue. It had been more than thirty years since he had been there! How time had flown!

Out of sheer curiosity, Avinash started walking towards his old university building from the wedding reception venue. It must have been around 10 p.m. It was a cold, foggy night. Avinash had always had this rather morbid fascination for exploring old buildings at night and could not resist the temptation again! Most old buildings develop very different characteristics at night and Avinash was keen on testing the environs of his old classrooms for anything of interest.

Avinash's relationship with his old university was rather complex. He had never been the quintessential insider in terms of academic pursuits and long-term ties with the teachers and his peers. But his worldview had definitely been influenced by certain aspects of his alma mater. Those days, the university had a vibrant energy, with a cross-flow of ideas, in spite of its predominantly leftist ethos. Most importantly, the university was a microcosm of the country in terms of its socio-economic composition and diversity of the student community. That, by itself, had been a living lesson in life for Avinash. Then, there was the other rare privilege offered by the university – one could be oneself without conforming to any dominant norm or narrative. The end result of all this was a degree of nostalgic fondness on the part of Avinash for the old institution. He had completely lost touch with the university and his old friends after he had joined the police service around thirty years ago.

As Avinash approached the old building, he was surprised to find that it looked exactly as it did thirty years ago! Strangely, he found the entrance to the main block open and a few lights were also switched on in the old classrooms. Somewhat hesitantly, he entered the building to find a lone clerk sitting under a dim light poring over some papers in what was once the old administration section. The clerk looked vaguely familiar, like someone dating back to Avinash's time, but he was puzzled to see that the clerk had not aged at all in all those years! Avinash rather gingerly approached him and introduced himself to the clerk as an old student who had passed out in 1986 after completing his MA course and that he had just come to see the old building out of curiosity. The clerk looked at Avinash rather incredulously and replied that the MA class of '86 cannot possibly have such an old student! Avinash was a little offended and told him that thirty-plus years is a long time and time does take its toll on everyone. The clerk, however, interjected curtly and said that the class of '86 is the current batch of second year MA students, and Avinash could not be in that class by any stretch of imagination! Avinash was a little taken aback by the clerk's rather rude and irrational behaviour and wondered whether the latter had consumed one too many that evening. They both somehow got talking to each other again, and the clerk pulled out a brand new register with the list of students of the class of '86. Avinash found that all the names in the list were accurate, including his! When he triumphantly pointed out this fact to the clerk, the latter got more annoyed and repeated his assertion that Avinash was talking illogically since none of the students in the class of '86 could be in their fifties, since it is the current second year MA class. Avinash's efforts to convince the clerk that the present year is 2016 fell on deaf ears and he did not press the matter any further for fear of further annoying the clerk.

Then Avinash tried to change the subject and asked the clerk about the present activities in the building. The clerk informed him that nothing has changed and the classes continued to be held there, the only difference being that all the classes were now being held in the evening shift! Also, he remarked that some professors were already present in the building, preparing for their lectures. Avinash expressed a keen desire to meet them and the clerk told him to go wherever he wanted to in the building and seek them out.

Avinash soon climbed the flight of stairs and reached the second floor of the old building and found a cold, poorly lit room with ancient dusty furniture and a group of people huddled together discussing something in quiet undertones. Avinash vaguely realized that all of them were his old teachers and he immediately recognized Prof P.K. Sen, who used to teach him International Law. Prof P.K. Sen did not look a day older than when Avinash had last seen him so many years ago! Very strange, Avinash thought, because Prof P.K. Sen was on the verge of retirement when he had taught Avinash's class! Avinash approached Prof Sen and introduced himself to the latter as his ex-student from the class of '86. The professor looked at him, hugely amused and guffawed that he had never had a student as old as Avinash, even among his Ph.D. students! "Obviously, you are mistaken, I could not have taught you," he remarked. Avinash repeated that he belonged to the class of '86 and Prof P.K. Sen replied, "Well, the class of '86 is the present class of second year MA students." He also told Avinash that, in fact, there was a class right now in progress for the MA students of '86 batch, and he could check that out for himself!

By now, Avinash was deeply confused and at the same time very intrigued. He got out of the old building and started walking towards his old classroom, which was outside the main block. From a distance, he could see that the old classroom was brilliantly lit, and he was almost blinded by the intensity of that light. As he approached the classroom, he experienced a very strange energy radiating from the light in the classroom, which he immediately experienced as the brilliant energy of youthful vitality and optimism. There was indeed a class in progress! Avinash was thoroughly shocked to find that the entire class of '86, including himself, were in that classroom! But it was as if the classroom was soundproof and he was unable to hear anything of the deliberations inside. Also, as he tried to enter the classroom, he felt as if he was unable to penetrate that invisible energy barrier of youthful vitality and optimism, due to his age. Avinash found the entire experience uncanny and rushed out of the premises, wondering whether he had mixed his drinks in the evening or if he was hallucinating!

As he came out of the building, Avinash was accosted by a security guard, who asked him what he was up to. Avinash told him that he had come for a wedding reception in the adjacent venue and was just exploring his old university building. The security guard informed him that the building now housed a government department and he should get out of the premises immediately. Before departing, Avinash enquired from the guard, whether the university classes still continued to be held in the evening shifts in that building. The security guard looked at Avinash in an oddly curious manner and offered no reply!

Avinash did not share this bizarre experience with anybody for fear of ridicule. But he made a mental note to narrate his strange experience to his friends from the class of '86, whenever they next met. But somehow, the occasion never arose.

It was a couple of years later, sometime in May 2018, that Avinash visited his old alma mater again, but in the new campus. On his way back in the evening from his office, Avinash impulsively decided to make a detour to the university campus. So much had changed in the new campus that he found it unrecognizable! When he got out of his car near the university library, it must have been around 7.30 p.m., and he was strangely drawn towards the 'big rocks' near the library, which used to be the venue for parties of all kinds in the university. As he approached the big rocks, he suddenly felt a distinct winter chill! The roads were all deserted and he could hear the distant chatter of people talking. Avinash suddenly saw a student emerging from the opposite direction, who was rather odd-looking; young and old at the same time, in an indeterminate sort of way. Avinash said hello to him and remarked that this area was so cold that it felt like December, even in the peak of summer! The student looked at Avinash quizzically and replied that it was indeed winter! He then asked Avinash whether he was going for the reunion of the MA class of 86 'taking place at the 'big rocks'. Avinash told him that he was not aware of any such reunion and asked him to elaborate. The student told Avinash that he was coming from there and had met some people there, who told him that the class of '86 was having a reunion after forty years. By now, Avinash was thoroughly puzzled and asked him 'What is the date today?' The student looked at him strangely and replied, 'Today is the 11 December 2026' and hastened his steps and disappeared along the road. By now, the 'big rocks' were clearly visible and Avinash found that there was indeed some kind of a party in progress. A shiver went down his spine when he saw that it was indeed the class of '86 and he was also present there! This time around, as he approached the group, the radiating energy he encountered was very different from the energy of youthful vitality and optimism of the old classroom. The present energy field was very dull, and he felt as if it was a mix of the waning powers of the five senses and a certain anxiety about the future. Avinash counted twenty-two of his old classmates including himself, wearing clothes he was sure he did not possess. But this time around, he could nearly break through the invisible energy barrier and watched the proceedings from close quarters for a while, without anybody noticing him. Soon, he left the big rocks, finding the whole experience eerie and inexplicable!

Avinash's two strange experiences in the old and new campuses of the university left him seriously wondering about his own mental state. He desperately wanted to hear some rational explanation for what he had experienced. Sometime in January 2019, as providence would have it, he attended a party hosted by his old friend, Professor Gopal Reddy, in his campus house in the old university. Gopal had been Avinash's classmate at the university and had gone on to become a professor there. Sometime during the party, Avinash came out of Professor Reddy's house to take in some fresh air and was delighted to discover that the next house belonged to Prof Anirudha Bose, who was his favourite teacher at the university. Professor Bose was just starting his career when Avinash was doing his post-graduation. Curious to meet his old professor, Avinash walked along and knocked at the door and was met by a young man in his early thirties, who introduced himself as Nachiketa Bose, son of Professor Anirudha Bose. As it transpired, the professor and his wife were out of town and

Nachiketa was alone in the house. Avinash got talking to him and was glad to know that Nachiketa had grown up on the campus and was now the Dean of the School of Fundamental Studies in a well-known foreign university. Nachiketa had a doctorate in physics as well as in philosophy, which Avinash thought was rather an odd combination! But Avinash soon realized that Nachiketa was an exceptionally brilliant young man. Rather hesitantly, Avinash narrated his two uncanny experiences in the university to Nachiketa and asked him if there was any rational explanation in physics for what he had experienced.

Nachiketa explained to Avinash that not just in physics, but even in philosophy, there are theories of multiple dimensions of time and space and he was exploring these very concepts in his post-doctoral research! Avinash found his exposition on the subject rather complex to understand, so Nachiketa simplified it for him by saying; 'Uncle, you see, you and I right now are in the present time and space continuum, but at the same time, there is a theoretical possibility, that we may also exist in a past or a future time and space continuum.' Nachiketa further explained that this is an emerging area of exploration and research in physics and hopefully, someday, there could be a scientifically proven explanation for Avinash's odd experience.

Avinash was much relieved after his conversation with Nachiketa, that at least, there was some vague scientific explanation behind his strange experiences. Nachiketa also told him in a strange tone, 'Uncle, do not regret the past or fear for the future, but fully embrace the present.' Avinash felt that this must be the philosopher in Nachiketa talking to him in an enigmatic manner.

Finally, before leaving, Avinash asked Nachiketa about his encounter with the clerk and the professors in the old university building, which felt very real to him. Nachiketa, rather mischievously replied, 'After all, where else can the old professors go after their teaching days are over?' Avinash heartily agreed and wished him well.

Back at Professor Gopal Reddy's party, Avinash told Reddy about his meeting with Nachiketa, Professor Bose's son, and remarked what a brilliant young man Nachiketa was. A strange and pained expression came over Professor Reddy's face as he replied, 'Avinash, that is not possible. Nachiketa passed away in a road accident in the United States in 2015, when he was teaching in a university there!'

The Small Boy who Loved Airports

Little Rongsen Ao, aged eight years, and his parents, Talimeren and Azine, lived in the small town of Bimapur, which among other things, also had a small airport. Talimeren owned a grocery shop in Bimapur, which afforded him a decent lower middle class living. The family had moved from their beautiful village home in the high mountains and green valleys of village Nokru to Bimapur town for better economic prospects. It was quite heart-wrenching for Talimeren and Azine to leave their lovely village of Nokru with its enchanting way of life, and settle down in the rather drab town of Bimapur. Both Talimeren and Azine had lived in a close-knit community in Nokru and it was an idyllic life. They worked on their family patch of land, foraged in the forests for greens and mushrooms, fished in the rivers for their daily needs and managed their small clutch of farm animals. Their life in the village was simple, but free of worries. Their happiest time there was during the annual festival of Moatsu, which lasted for three days. It was a time for everyone in Nokru to renew friendships and exchange gifts. Both Talimeren and Azine had been educated in the nearby missionary school, which had given them an exposure and knowledge of the outside world beyond their own little village. This had fired an ambition in both of them to offer the best possible opportunity in life to little Rongsen and hence, they had moved to Bimapur town. Talimeren and Azine were both aspirational and hoped for a better life beyond their little village. Rongsen, with his twinkling eyes and chubby cheeks, was their only child. Rongsen was a lovely child; full of life and curiosity and very adept at computers at such a young age. The doting parents fondly hoped that he would study well and become a computer engineer one day. The parents had indulged his fancy and even bought him a tablet, which was his constant companion.

Then suddenly, around a year after the family had moved to Bimapur town, Rongsen started falling ill regularly. He started developing breathing problems, found it difficult to walk, and felt weak even when not doing any physical activity. The local doctors in Bimapur could not diagnose his medical condition. Talimeren took him for treatment to a nearby city with better hospitals. After extensive checks, Rongsen was diagnosed with an illness known as muscular dystrophy. The doctors told Talimeren that it was a very serious disorder which caused progressive degeneration and breakdown of skeletal muscles. There was no complete cure for this condition and it could only be managed to some extent with medication and certain therapies. To determine the type of muscular dystrophy, the hospital conducted Rongsen's muscle biopsy, and the results were not encouraging. He was diagnosed with the DMD variety which was deemed by the doctors as more severe. The doctors in the city felt that perhaps Rongsen's condition was not diagnosed soon enough, given the absence of good medical facilities in Bimapur. There had been a history of this illness in Talimeren's family. Little Rongsen's condition quickly worsened, and he became wheelchair bound, unable to walk, much to the sorrow of his family.

Talimeren and Azine were simple, god-fearing people, ready to sacrifice everything for Rongsen's treatment. Unfortunately, the doctors informed them that in most DMD cases, the life span of the patient gets greatly curtailed. But the devoted parents that they were, Talimeren and Azine refused to even contemplate such an eventuality for their only child. They decided to give him the best possible medical treatment. The treatment of Rongsen's condition necessitated frequent visits to the nearby city with the requisite medical facilities. The family used to fly often from Bimapur airport and that was how Avinash came to know of this family and about Rongsen's illness.

Avinash, those days, was involved in the supervision of aviation security. One day he received an e-mail on the passenger grievance portal from Azine, complaining about the travelling difficulties for her son Rongsen, who was wheelchair bound, due to the airport security protocols. Avinash had done many kinds of policing jobs during his long career, but had found aviation security to be a different kettle of fish. The overriding nature of this job was sensitivity; both in terms of ensuring foolproof security at the airports and in handling the passengers with the requisite soft skills, which were very different from normal policing requirements. The security processes at the airports had to be compliant with international protocols so that there were uniform standards across the world. At the same time, passenger handling required patience of high order since the passengers were very demanding during their interactions with the security personnel. Avinash had learnt early that an ideal system was the one in which the passenger turnover was quick and the security checks were conducted professionally. This demanded high levels of competence from the security personnel at airports, which required constant training and supervision, which Avinash tried his best to ensure. Also, every day, there were specially-abled passengers, who had to be handled with even greater sensitivity and under special protocols. So, when Avinash received Azine's message on the grievance redressal portal, he was already grappling with the issue of formulating new protocols to ease the air travel experience of passengers on wheelchairs and also those fitted with prosthetic limbs.

The existing security protocols for persons with disabilities mandated a thorough screening of all the wheelchairs or the prosthetics, as the case may be, to rule out hidden explosives or concealed weapons in the components and the hollow parts of such devices. This caused terrible inconvenience to passengers with disabilities, as they had to get up from the wheelchair to get it screened, or had to remove the prosthetics for x-ray screening, which was very humiliating. Moreover, these devices were specially aligned and calibrated to meet the specific physical needs of the person concerned and even the slightest mishandling during the security checks disturbed the calibration and caused much discomfort to the passenger subsequently. Some of the security staff also lacked the required sensitivity while conducting such checks at times. The airport security ecosystem was in the process of formulating new protocols to ease the distress of air passengers with disabilities when

Azine's complaint was received. Avinash had decided, in consultation with the regulatory authorities, that minimum inconvenience should be caused to such passengers during security checks and a modality was devised to screen them without forcing them to get out of the wheelchairs or to remove their prosthetics, unless there were very compelling circumstances. Avinash knew that the dissemination of such information and the training of the airport security staff in implementing the new protocols takes time. There was also a tendency among the security staff to check everyone indiscriminately, to be on the safer side.

When Avinash received Azine's e-mail, his office got in touch with her and thereafter, instructed Inspector Pradeep Chaudhary, who was in charge of airport security at Bimapur airport, to contact Rongsen's family and attend to their problem. It transpired that Rongsen's plight was similar to that of the other wheelchair bound passengers. The child's mobility was now severely restricted, and he had to be lifted physically from the wheelchair every time he passed through the security check. It was a very intimidating and an inconvenient experience for the child. Also, the impersonal and intrusive nature of the security checks in general had made little Rongsen rather afraid of going to the airports.

Inspector Pradeep Chaudhary was an old aviation security hand. But he had started his aviation security stint on the wrong foot, without intending to do so. He hailed from a particular state with a typical style of conversational inflexion and his natural style was construed as rudeness by many air passengers. He always tried his best to change his conversational style, but with mixed and sometimes hilarious results. Pradeep Chaudhary had spent all his working life at airports and had grown to love the ambience of his workplace. He was always on friendly terms with the airport employees, the pilots, the air hostesses, and other stakeholders at the airport. He loved his job and liked being at the terminals. For him, the glitz and the energy of the airport terminal was an escape from the problems of the real world. He had started his career as a baggage screener, which is a horrendously monotonous job. Every day, he had to scan hundreds of bags that passed through the X-ray machines. He had to identify prohibited items like explosives, weapons, knives, drugs, etc., in those bags and ensure that they do not get into the aircraft. The images of many objects on the X-ray screen are often unclear, and they have to be interpreted accurately. A single mistake by the screener could result in a serious security breach; the plane can even get hijacked or sabotaged since the aviation sector is always on the radar of terrorists. Pradeep Chaudhary had come through successfully in his career without any mishaps after long years as a screener and was now in a supervisory role.

Immediately after receiving instructions from Avinash's office, Pradeep Chaudhary got in touch with Azine and her husband Talimeren and requested them to inform him the next time they were flying from Bimapur airport with Rongsen. That marked the beginning of a warm friendship between Pradeep Chaudhary and Rongsen's family.

Bimapur was a very sensitive airport when it came to security; the region having had an old history of insurgency. But Pradeep Chaudhary got the background checks of Talimeren's family conducted and assessed that they posed little or no security threat at all. He felt it was highly unlikely that anyone would misuse Rongsen's powered wheelchair to surreptitiously plant explosives or weapons, given the family's background. The new aviation security protocols had enabled field officers like Pradeep Chaudhary to conduct security screening of wheelchair bound passengers not deemed to be a security threat, in less intrusive ways. Pradeep Chaudhary also requested his colleagues at other airports, through which Rongsen travelled, to ease the child's travel woes.

So, little Rongsen's travels through the airports now become a breeze! Very soon, he befriended the security staff and everyone else at the Bimapur airport. Pradeep Chaudhary sometimes even allowed Rongsen to watch the X-ray screening process of baggage from a distance, and Rongsen learnt to identify screen images of various objects fairly accurately! Perhaps with his illness getting more acute, visits to the airports now became an escape route from the grim realities of life for little Rongsen. Bimapur airport was very small and did not have the usual bustle and glamour of the larger airports. But for Rongsen, Bimapur airport was a place of happiness and he would goad his parents to go in early, roam all over the terminal, play with the sniffer dogs and chat with his good friend Pradeep Chaudhary. In fact, before every trip, Talimeren would call Pradeep and inform him, so that the latter could be present at the airport, even if it was a day off for him. Even when he was not travelling, Rongsen used to constantly bombard Pradeep with messages and information about various matters from his tablet. Usually, they were jigsaw puzzles and trick questions, but sometimes, Rongsen would share a lot of material with Pradeep on matters related to afterlife! Rongsen was very precocious and would also do research on the latest security gadgetry for airports and share such information with Pradeep, much to the latter's astonishment! Pradeep Chaudhary would occasionally visit the modest Talimeren household and partake of the delicious Sunday lunch and also check on Rongsen's well-being. It was an unusual and close friendship between a middle-aged man with a strange accent and an eight-year-old child.

However, soon, Rongsen's condition started worsening. The medical expenses and the air travel were proving difficult for the parents to bear, but the family and friends of Talimeren and Azine in Nokru village rallied around them and contributed generously towards Rongsen's medical care. Despite all their efforts, slowly, the illness was telling on the child's cheerful nature and he was becoming more withdrawn and quieter. Any physical activity was now proving to be difficult for him.

This time around, Rongsen had not come to the airport for more than a month. Even the regular relay of messages from Rongsen's tablet to Pradeep were infrequent. Pradeep had been thinking of calling Talimeren to enquire about Rongsen's health, but the past few days had witnessed incidents of IED explosions in certain places around Bimapur and the airport was on high alert. There were intelligence reports that the airport may also be targeted by the miscreants. On that particular day, Pradeep Chaudhary had completed his morning rounds of the airport and as he was settling down in his office, he received a rather curious message from Rongsen that there were two suspicious bags in the airport terminal, which needed to be cleared immediately. Pradeep Chaudhary was quite used to prank messages from Rongsen, but since the airport was already on high alert, he decided to investigate the matter. A thorough search of the airport indeed resulted in the discovery of two unclaimed bags outside the security hold area of the terminal! Upon checking, the sniffer dogs confirmed the possible presence of explosives in those bags. Pradeep Chaudhary immediately summoned the bomb disposal unit, which found that both the bags had IEDs with timer devices! After following the necessary protocols, the IEDs were defused and a major incident of bomb blast at the Bimapur airport was averted. The bomb unit determined that the quantity of explosives in the IED was sufficient to cause major damage to life and property at the airport, had it gone off.

Pradeep Chaudhary was quite intrigued at how little Rongsen could have got the information of the suspect baggage and decided to call Talimeren to enquire about the matter. At the other end of the line, Pradeep Chaudhary found Talimeren completely distraught, who informed him that Rongsen had succumbed to his illness the previous night and passed away! Pradeep Chaudhary was speechless with shock, but decided that no useful purpose would be served by following up with Talimeren on Rongsen's mysterious message, since in the final analysis, the little child's odd action, however inexplicable, had protected his beloved airport and his friends from harm. But nothing prepared Pradeep Chaudhary for the astonishment of a subsequent message from Rongsen's tablet a little while later; an emoji of thumbs up and goodbye!

Pradeep Chaudhary has since moved out of Bimapur airport, but firmly believes that Bimapur airport does not need security anymore, since a chubby little guardian angel takes care of it!

Bote Aiyappa of the Sacred Grove

Avinash had this rather odd habit of going for late-night walks whenever he visited his village, Bettagrama. He usually commenced his walk from his house after dinner in a southerly direction towards the Kadpole river, also known as the 'wild' river. It was not a very long walk, in fact only a little over half a kilometre or so. He was usually armed with a torch and a stick as a precaution against snakes and wild animals. The thing he liked about this walk was the complete absence of human beings en route. He also found it amusing to watch the reaction of the odd late-night motorists, when they saw this strange figure in a kurta pyjama, an unusual attire for these parts, armed with a torch and a stick, on a deserted road! The motorists invariably sped away rather hastily in considerable trepidation. Over time, the local villagers also came to notice this odd habit of Avinash, which was unconvincingly explained to them by Avinash's family as his fitness regime. Avinash found these walks very interesting and very different each time. On dark clear nights, the sky was brilliant with millions of stars shining brightly and he felt as if the earth was a different planet with no civilization. On moonlit nights, the experience was ethereal, with the dappled interplay of light and shadow cast by the old trees on both sides of the road. Then there were misty nights; the mist came suddenly as if from nowhere and also disappeared suddenly without a warning!

Once Avinash had reached the Kadpole river, he would stand on the bridge and watch the water rippling over the ancient boulders. It was a pleasing sound and on full moon nights, the water sometimes sparkled like a thousand diamonds! There was not much wildlife left in Bettagrama village, except itinerant elephant herds, but occasionally, Avinash would hear the strange wailing of some night bird or the eerie howling of a jackal pack, which made the walk all the more mysterious.

Beyond the bridge over the Kadpole river, the boundary of Bettagrama village ceased and the area of Kottageri village started. Somehow, like a territorial animal, Avinash never ventured out into Kottageri during his night walks. During his childhood, he had listened to stories of strange paranormal activities in Kottageri from the farm helps, and it was imprinted on his brain even now.

Even during the daytime, Avinash had found Kottageri village rather desolate and unwelcome. The public road was always covered with leaf litter, as if no vehicle had passed over the road for a long time. There were very few houses in the village and the occasional wayfarer Avinash encountered, looked sullen and rather unfriendly. As one crossed the Kadpole bridge and entered Kottageri village, the first sight which greeted the onlooker was a strange abandoned property. Apparently, the building had once been a tourist resort which was shut down a long time ago after a client had died in the premises due to unknown reasons. Nobody in Bettagrama knew who was the owner of the resort or who had died there.

One particular morning, many years ago, Avinash had quietly explored the abandoned resort and found it very intriguing. The property was completely overrun by tall grass, typical to the banks of Kadpole. There were a few cottages, a huge dining room and a kitchen. Strangely, although the buildings were all dilapidated, the furniture, the fittings and the paintings on the walls were all still intact! The dining table had a neat row of plates and cutlery as if a group of people were ready for dinner. Even the beds in some of the cottages looked as if they had been slept in, just the previous night! Then, there were snakes crawling all over the property and even inside the buildings. Avinash had beaten a hasty retreat and never ventured out there again.

He had heard the local lore from the villagers of Bettagrama that the abandoned resort was a regular meeting place for the departed souls of all surrounding villages! Some villagers even claimed that they had heard peals of female laughter emanating from the property when they had gone out at night on some errand or the other. So Avinash always gave a wide berth to the place during his nightly peregrinations.

Avinash also occasionally walked in the night in the opposite direction, towards the foothills of Balya Betta, the large hillock which was the landmark of Bettagrama village. This stretch of the road had more homesteads and was not nearly as lonely. Avinash sometimes encountered the odd village drunkard on this stretch, returning home furtively from his daily indulgences. He usually walked till the devakaad or the sacred grove, which was a small patch of forest in the village, where cutting of trees was completely prohibited. The sacred grove was also home to a small shrine of a demi-god known locally as Bote Aiyappa. Although Bote Aiyappa was revered as the Lord-of-the-hunt, he was considered the guardian angel of the sacred grove and it was widely believed in Bettagrama that he did not take kindly to hunting of wild animals or cutting of trees in his patch of the forest. The villagers sometimes made offerings of food and flowers to the shrine, which was actually nothing more than a large stone under an ancient tree. But the practice of making offerings to Bote Aiyappa by the villagers had greatly reduced over the years due to general apathy in Bettagrama. Avinash himself remembered that he had made an offering of wildflowers a very long time ago, when he was just a child.

It was sometime in early 2020 that the first rumours of tiger movement started in Bettagrama village. Tigers were unheard here. There was the occasional rare sighting of leopards or elephant herds in Balya Betta, but never of tigers. Soon, eyewitness accounts started emerging. Many people reported seeing four tigers together, sometimes on the foothills of Balya Betta, sometimes around the sacred grove, and occasionally on the banks of the Kadpole river! Soon tongues started wagging in Bettagrama that Bote Aiyappa was unhappy with the villagers due to his neglect and had unleashed the tigers upon them! Also, someone had recently cut an ancient tree in the sacred grove and decamped with the timber, which the villagers believed, must have angered Bote Aiyappa! But soon, simpler explanations emerged. It was informed by the forest department that a tigress with three cubs had moved out of a nearby reserve forest and taken up residence in and around Bettagrama village. However, despite the frequent sightings of the tigers and their pug marks all over the village, there were no attacks on villagers or killings of domestic animals. It was a mystery to everyone what the tigers preyed upon. Bettagrama and the surrounding villages had a decent wild boar population, and it was believed to be their main source of food. It was only in the beginning of 2022 that isolated cattle killings commenced, not in Bettagrama itself, but in the surrounding areas. Strangely, there was not a single cattle kill in Bettagrama village. However, the villagers soon started complaining about the activities of the marauding tigers and the forest officials attempted to tranquilize them for translocation, but without any success. Three tame elephants of the forest department scoured the area for many days, but could not locate the tigers. The forest officials were of the view that by now, the three tiger cubs had grown to become sub-adults and were trying to carve out their own territories and preying upon cattle, in the absence of other viable prey.

Then the first human kill happened in Kottageri village. An estate worker was killed while he was relieving himself, but his body had been left untouched. The forest officials believed it was an accidental killing, but the villagers were not convinced and were very furious now. The terror of the four tigers soon gripped and spread in and around the villages of Bettagrama and all agricultural activities stopped completely. The villagers avoided venturing out of their homes after dusk and it appeared as if an undeclared curfew had been ordered in the entire area. Then, suddenly, the tiger sightings around Bettagrama mysteriously stopped sometime in the middle of 2022 and the villagers breathed a collective sigh of relief! It was believed by the forest department that all the tigers had gone back to the nearby reserve forest and carved out their own territories. But every three months or so, large saucer sized pug-marks were seen all over Bettagrama village, but there were no actual tiger sightings. The forest officials now believed that Bettagrama village had become part of a regular territorial beat of an adult tigress, the mother of the three cubs.

Avinash had heard of all these developments and was very excited initially. Tigers in Bettagrama! All his life, he had visited many nature reserves searching for the ever-elusive tiger. Now there were tigers in his own village! But his feelings became far more complex upon seeing the impact of the presence of these tigers on the life of the villagers. It was not easy for the villagers to coexist with tigers in an agricultural landscape, with no viable wild prey base for the felines. There was always the risk of a sudden encounter, which could turn fatal. But inexplicably, Bettagrama village continued to remain free of any cattle kills or accidental encounters with people, in spite of the periodic movement of the animal!

Soon, Avinash was on one of his rare short visits to Bettagrama again. But this time around, his entire family advised him against any reckless night walks. However, on the last night of his visit, he could not resist the temptation anymore. This time around, he decided to walk towards the direction of the sacred grove, which he thought was the safer route, and commenced his walk earlier than usual as a precaution. The moon was in its first phase and the visibility was good. Avinash walked along the road and soon crossed the sacred grove, but decided on some impulse to turn back since something made him uneasy. That was when he first heard a low growl emanating from the undergrowth not too far away! Cursing his own foolhardy behaviour, he retraced his steps hastily to reach home quickly, but the growls started growing louder and louder. As Avinash neared the sacred grove again, he could faintly discern the massive shape of a tiger, perhaps ten to fifteen metres behind him, seemingly intent on following him purposefully! Now Avinash was fairly panic-stricken, sweating very profusely and getting slightly disoriented, since home was still a fair distance away.

As Avinash crossed the shrine of Bote Aiyappa in the sacred grove, suddenly there was a penetrating, ear-splitting scream from the bowels of the forest patch, which sounded like 'Yeaeeee phoooah!! Yeaeeee phoooah!' Avinash froze in sheer terror, since no human being could have made such a blood curdling sound and the tiger also seemed to have heard it and bounded away in the opposite direction, as if in fear. Avinash wondered if it was one of the village drunkards who had screamed in such an unearthly manner, but did not bother to wait and find out! The scream actually sounded like 'you get lost' in the local dialect, but with an almost non-human timbre! Anyway, the tiger was now gone and Avinash quickly reached home, greatly relieved. He narrated the incident to his family members and was roundly castigated by all of them for his stupidity in not heeding to their earlier warnings about walking in the night with tigers prowling around. However, Avinash carefully avoided any mention of the unearthly scream he had heard in the sacred grove. The next morning, while leaving Bettagrama, Avinash made it a point to stop at the shrine of Bote Aiyappa after so many years and offered a shower of fresh flowers to the demi-god and thanked him.

Avinash has recently learnt that the saucer-sized pug marks of the tigress have been seen again all over Bettagrama village, but this time around accompanied by three more sets of tiny pug marks! The villagers are wondering if there is trouble brewing again in Bettagrama. However, Avinash feels that it is very unlikely that any harm will come to the village with Bote Aiyappa looking after the scheme of things in the village.

Now that Avinash has retired from police service, he is looking forward to many more walking adventures in Bettagrama, regardless of his family's apprehensions!

Acknowledgements

I owe a debt of gratitude to my wife Sandhya for going through my stories and suggesting improvements. Also, to my son Nikhil for being stoic, whenever I boasted about my potential magnum opus!

I thank my parents, M.S. Appaya and Prem Appaya for believing that I can do many things well. My sisters, Kshama and Kripa, as well as nieces and nephews – Ananya & Anindya, Mrinal & Chirag – seemed to have genuinely liked the stories set in Bettagrama village; so a thank you to all of them.

Most importantly, I am indebted to Mrs Sangita Chaudhary for editing my stories initially, and cutting out all the verbiage.

Also, sincere thanks to my energetic and resourceful literary agent, Anish Chandy for putting me through to Srishti publishers. Arup Bose, Stuti, Alisha and the team at Srishti have done a marvellous job of polishing my raw material; thank you for the professionalism.

Last but not least, a big thank you to Srinivas and Shailendra, my PAs for the tireless turnover of corrected copies without complaints!